Herbert of Cherbury

The Poems of Lord Herbert of Cherbury

Herbert of Cherbury

The Poems of Lord Herbert of Cherbury

ISBN/EAN: 9783744711777

Printed in Europe, USA, Canada, Australia, Japan

Cover: Foto ©Andreas Hilbeck / pixelio.de

More available books at **www.hansebooks.com**

THE

POEMS OF LORD HERBERT

OF CHERBURY

EDITED

WITH AN INTRODUCTION

BY

JOHN CHURTON COLLINS

LONDON
CHATTO AND WINDUS, PICCADILLY
1881

LONDON :

PRINTED BY STRANGEWAYS AND SONS, TOWER STREET,

UPPER ST. MARTIN'S LANE, W.C.

I INSCRIBE

THIS LITTLE VOLUME

TO MY FRIEND

WILLIAM BAPTISTE SCOONES,

AN

IMPERFECT EXPRESSION

OF

ESTEEM AND AFFECTION.

PREFACE.

WHETHER the Poems, which are here for the first time prefented in a modern drefs, be of intrinfic value the reader will foon determine for himfelf. I have at leaft brought Herbert before the Court; and I have, I hope, fecured him a fair hearing. Henceforth he will not be condemned unheard.

With regard to the text, I have adhered with fcrupulous fidelity to that of the original edition; and I have collated the only two copies to which I could obtain accefs—the copy in the Britifh Mufeum, and the copy in the Bodleian Library at Oxford—without, however, difcovering any variety of readings. My principal difficulty has been with the punctuation, on which, of courfe, the fenfe of paffages frequently depends; and for this I have often had no guidance from the original, which teems with palpable errors. The fpelling has **alfo** been carefully revifed, and though it has been for **the** moft part modernifed, I have thought it well **to** retain, in fome cafes, the older forms, fo as **to** preferve the flavour **of** archaifm. Obvious mifprints have been filently corrected. In two paffages only *I* have ventured to alter the text, and they both occur **in** 'The Idea.' In the feventh line the original reads 'bear,' which, as it makes no fenfe, and breaks the rhyme, I alter into 'bar.' Again, in the laft line, 'whence' is fubftituted for 'when.' And for this reafon. Herbert is alluding to the Platonic doctrine of ideas, and it is much more natural to fuppofe that *he* would fpeak **of** an idea whence *the form began than* of **an idea** when *the* form began. Though he is **miftaken in** fuppofing that the Platonic ideas admit of application to particular individuals, he was evidently acquainted with the '*Timæus*' **and with** the '*Republic.*'

J. CHURTON COLLINS.

5 *King's Bench Walk, Temple.*

CONTENTS.

b

INTRODUCTION.

LORD HERBERT of Cherbury is one of the moſt interesting, and in many reſpects one of the moſt essentially original characters, in our Literary Hiſtory. At once a philoſopher and a politician, a man of the world and a man of letters, it was his lot to flouriſh at a criſis of no ordinary importance in philoſophy, in politics, in literature. His youth was paſſed in the world of Hooker, Sydney, and Spenſer. Before he died Hobbes had written the *Elementa Philoſophica de Cive*, Barclay had publiſhed his *Argenis*, and Butler was collecting materials for *Hudibras*. He was a child of eight when Elizabeth addreſſed the ſoldiers at Tilbury Fort, and he lived to ſee Charles the Firſt betrayed by the Scots to the Engliſh Commiſſioners. He was the friend of Donne and Ben Jonſon ; he was the correſpondent of Grotius and Gaſſendi. He thus ſtood midway between two great eras, moving in both. In temper he belonged to the era of the Renaiſſance, in intellect he belonged to the era of Des Cartes and Hobbes. His own ſervices to literature

were important. His *De Veritate*, if it did not do much
for the advancement of metaphyfical philofophy, was the
work of a fearlefs, vigorous, and independent thinker ; a
work which exercifed confiderable influence on the pro-
grefs of **Free** Enquiry, **and was the** firft attempt made,
in this country at leaft, to reduce Deifm to a fyftem.
His *Life and Reign of Henry VIII.* is an admirable piece
of hiftorical compofition. His *Expeditio Buckinghami
Ducis in Ream Infulam* is the beft account we have of
that unhappy adventure ; and his *Autobiography* is, if ever
autobiography was, a treafure for all time.

Thus interefting by his furroundings, thus important
in himfelf, **we** are the more attracted towards him becaufe
of the fulnefs with which we are acquainted with the
incidents of his perfonal hiftory. We know him as we
know no other man **of that** age. Never fince Jerome
Cardan laid bare for the world's infpection the innermoft
fecrets of his being, never fince Cellini told the ftory
of his ftrange viciffitudes, **never** fince Montaigne took
Europe into his confidence, had fuch a record as Herbert
has left **us** been committed to paper. Whether he in-
tended his fingular confeffions for publication may well
be doubted. He tells us himfelf that **they** were written
for the inftruction of **his** defcendents, and to enable
him to review his paft career, that he might reform
what was amifs if fuch reformation were poffible, that

he might comfort himfelf with the memory of whatever virtuous actions he might have done, and that he
might make his peace with God. In the courfe of this
review he not only narrates the adventures which he
had encountered on his way through life, but he enters
into minute particulars relating to his writings and
fpeculations—his ftruggles with his paffions, his ftruggles
with his reafon : he gives us his opinions on education, on
the conduct of life, on religion. And he is to all appearance unreferved. His frailties **are not** concealed, and
they are many ; **but** we feel that he has, on the whole,
gained rather than loft by a fcrutiny which few, indeed, of
our erring race could court with impunity. Nor is this
all. **It is** the portrait of a man with features eminently
ftriking and peculiar, whofe ways were never the ways of
common men, whofe thoughts were not the thoughts
either of his predeceffors or contemporaries. Nothing,
therefore, which Herbert has left us can be without importance ; for, whatever be its intrinfic value, it is the
product of an original mind developing itfelf under ex-
ceptionally interefting hiftorical conditions.

The world has long **done juftice to** his profe writings.
It is the object of the prefent volume to vindicate his
title to a place among Englifh poets. I have certainly no
wifh to be numbered among thofe gentlemen whofe in-
difcriminating induftry continues **year** after year to load

our libraries with treafures better hidden. I have no wifh
to rob Oblivion of its legitimate prey. Some of Lord
Herbert's poems are, I freely admit, not worth refufcitation,
but many of them, or portions at leaft of many of them,
feem to me authentic poetry. In almoft all of them we
find originality and vigour, however fantaftic the con-
ception, however rough the execution. But were their
merits even lefs than they are, no cultivated man could
regard them with indifference. The name of their writer
would be a fufficient paffport to indulgent attention. We
treafure the verfes of the authors of the *Nicomachæan
Ethics,* and of the *Novum Organon,* though Ariftotle has
no claim to **a** place among the Pleiad, **or** Bacon to a
place befide Jonfon or Donne.

In my eftimate of Lord Herbert's poems I have
hitherto ftood alone. His biographers and critics are
unanimous in ignoring or condemning them. Antony
Wood paffes them by without comment. Horace Walpole
merely mentions them **in** his Catalogue **of** Herbert's
Works. Neither Grainger nor the author of the life in
the *Biographie Univerfelle* have anything to fay for them.
Park, in a note on Walpole's *Life of Herbert,* coldly
fpeaks of ' Lord Herbert's fcarce volume of metaphyfical
love verfes, ingenious but unnatural, platonic in fentiment,
but frequently grofs in expreffion, and marked by an
eccentricity which pervaded the life and charaĉter of their

author;' and thefe remarks have been greedily copied into
fucceffive editions of bibliographic manuals, reprints, and
the like. **Ellis,** in his *Specimens of Englifh Poetry*, is ftill
lefs favourable in his verdict, boldly obferving that young
Herbert 'fhowed more piety than tafte in publifhing his
father's poems.' The author of an article on the *Autobiography* in the *Retrofpective Review* contents himfelf
with remarking that Lord Herbert is often 'both rugged
and obfcure in his verfes,' and 'was much more fitted to
wield the fword than the lyre.' They have no place in
the *Selections* of Headley. Even Campbell, who can
find a niche for Heminge and Picke, has no corner for
Herbert. **M.** Charles de Rémufat, in his interefting and
valuable treatife, *Lord Herbert of Cherbury, fa Vie et
fes Œuvres*, expreffes fimilar opinions : 'Ses poéfies
anglaies, publiées par fon fecond fils, font d'un genre
moins ferieux'—(he has been fpeaking, and fpeaking de-
preciatingly, of Herbert's Latin poems)—' Quelques unes
font ingenieufes, la plufpart obfcures ; l'amour en eft le
fujet ordinaire, un amour platonique, exprimé cependant
avec plus de recherche que délicateffe.' It is curious that
they fhould have efcaped the notice of Sir Egerton Brydges,
who has not, fo far as I can difcover, made any allufion
to them. And this is the more remarkable, as he was
particularly interefted in the hiftory of the Herbert family,
and was the firft editor of the poems of William Herbert,

third Earl of Pembroke. When he obferved in the preface to his reprint of the Earl's poems that 'to fuffer them
to lie longer in oblivion would be to defraud an illuftrious
family of its greateft ornaments,' he made a remark which
would be far more applicable to the prefent volume.
Whatever opinion may be formed of Lord Herbert's
merits as a poet, there can be no queftion as to his
fuperiority to his kinfman.

It is ftrange that in his *Autobiography* Lord Herbert
makes no mention of his Poems, the exiftence of
which feems not to have been fufpected by any of
his diftinguifhed contemporaries. They were evidently
jotted down in moments of leifure, as occafion offered.
Some of them were the work of his youth, fome of his
middle age; the laft was written four years before his
death. This we gather from the dates prefixed to many
of them, the earlieft date being Auguft 1608, the lateft
October 1664. The biographers affure us that many of
thefe poems had appeared in print during Herbert's lifetime, and are to be found in the poetical collections of
the period. For thefe collections I have fearched in vain.
I doubt, I muft own, the truth of the ftatement, and fufpect
that it has been loofely copied, without any attempt to
afcertain its correctnefs, from Antony Wood; and I am
the more inclined to believe this becaufe they have faithfully
repeated one grofs blunder of Wood's—a blunder which

would at once have been rectified by confulting the work
to which **Wood** refers. It is this, and it is fignificant :
In the third volume of his *Athenæ Oxonienfes* (edition
Blifs, p. 242) Wood fays : ' Other of Lord Herbert's
poems I have feen in the books of other authors occafionally written, particularly in that of Jofhua Sylvefter,
entitled *Lacrymæ Lacrymarum,* 1613.' This affertion is
repeated by Walpole, by Sir Walter Scott in the Pre-
fatory Memoir to Lord Herbert's *Autobiography*, publifhed at Edinburgh in 1809, by the editor of Murray's
reprint of the *Life*, and by all the bibliographers. Now
there is not a line of Lord Herbert's to be found in
Sylvefter's work. What Wood was thinking of was no
doubt the *Elegy for the Prince* (fee Poems, page 33),
which certainly was publifhed during Herbert's lifetime,
but which appeared, not in Sylvefter's *Lacrymæ Lacrymarum,* but in a collection entitled *Sundry Funeral Elegies
on the Untimely Death of the Moft Excellent Prince Henry*,
compofed by feveral hands, 1613. However this may
be, the poems made their appearance in a collected form
in 1665, nearly feventeen years after Herbert's death ;
and were, as we learn from the Preface, given to the
world by Henry Herbert, his youngeft fon. Of thefe
poems there appears to have been only one edition.
The volume is now extremely rare ; indeed, it is one of
the rareft known to bibliographers.

The reader will at once difcover that Herbert belongs, like his brother, to that fchool of poets whofe characteriftics have been fo admirably analyfed by Johnfon—the Metaphyfical or Phantaftic School. This fingular fect firft appeared during the latter years of Elizabeth's reign. Their origin is popularly afcribed to Dr. Donne, though it would in truth be more correct to fay that in the poetry of Donne their peculiarities of fentiment and expreffion are moft confpicuoufly illuftrated. They owed their origin, indeed, not to the influence of Donne, but to the fpirit of the age. In all eras of great creative energy poetry paffes neceffarily through two ftages : in the firft ftage, imagination predominates ; in the fecond, reflection. **In the** firft ftage, men feel more than they think ; in the fecond, they think **more** than they feel. If a literature run its natural courfe, we may predict with abfolute certainty that mere rhetoric will **ufurp** the place of the eloquent language of the paffions, that fancy will be fubftituted for imagination, **and that there** will ceafe to be any neceffary correfpondence between the emotions and the intellect. This ftage was not completely attained till the age of Cowley. In the poetry of Donne we find the tranfition between the two ftages marked with fingular precifion. Some of his poems remind us of the richeft and frefheft work of the Elizabethan age ; in many of them he out-Cowleys Cowley himfelf. But his work was not the work, in any fenfe, of a creator. He contributed no new elements, either to thought or to diction. What he did was to unite the vicious peculiarities of others, to indulge habitually in what they indulged in only occafionally. He was not, for example, the firft to fubftitute philofophical reflection for poetic feeling, as his contemporaries, Samuel Daniel, Sir John Davies, and Fulke Greville, were fimultaneoufly engaged in doing the fame thing. He was not the firft to indulge in abufe of wit, in fanciful fpeculations, in extravagant imagery, or in grotefque eccentricities of expreffion. But, in addition to uniting thefe vices, he carried them further than any of his predeceffors or contemporaries had done, and, aided by the fpirit of the age, he fucceeded in making them popular. It would not, perhaps, be faying too much to fay that no fingle author contributed more to the foundation of the Metaphyfical School than Jofhua Sylvefter, whofe tranflation of Du Bartas preceded the ' metaphyfical' poems of Donne, and was probably as favourite a work with Donne as it certainly was with moft of the young poets of that age. The ftyle of Donne is, however, marked by certain diftinctive peculiarities which no intelligent critic would be likely to miftake, and his influence on contemporary poetry was unqueftionably confiderable. Lord Herbert appears to have been the earlieft of his difciples. Indeed, moft of the poems in Herbert's collection in which the influence of Donne is moſt perceptible, had been written, as the dates ſhow, long before the poems of Donne were given to the world. But he was, we know, perſonally acquainted with Donne, and Donne, like many of the poets of that age, was in the habit of circulating copies of his poems among private friends.* His acquaintance with his maſter commenced, no doubt, while he was ſtill a ſtudent at Univerſity College; for we learn from Walton's *Life of George Herbert* that when Mrs. Herbert was living with her ſon Edward at Oxford Donne arrived there on a viſit, and became, during her reſidence at Oxford, one of her moſt valued friends and adviſers. His beautiful poem entitled the *Autumnal* was written in honour of Mrs. Herbert. As Herbert was then a youth of eighteen, and Donne a man of upwards of forty, it is not unreaſonable to ſuppoſe that Donne aſſiſted both in moulding the youth's taſtes and in directing his ſtudies.

Where Herbert moſt reminds us of Donne is not

---

* Dr. Groſart, in his laborious and inſtructive account of Donne and his writings, tells us that ſeveral of Donne's deſcriptive and ſatirical poems were in circulation among friends certainly before 1614, and that ſome of his lyrics were in circulation before 1613. (See his remarks on his edition of Donne, vol. ii., *Eſſay on the Life and Writings of Donne,* pp. xxxi. and xxxii.)

fo much in his lyrics as in his poems written in the heroic meafures; in the two fatires, for example, in the verfes 'To his Miftrefs for her True Picture,' in the elegy on Donne himfelf. The poem alfo entitled ' The Idea ' is very much in his friend's vein, as well as written in a meafure which Donne perhaps invented, and which was certainly a favourite with him. The numerous poems dedicated to the praife of dark beauty were perhaps fuggefted by Donne's verfes *To a Lady of Dark Complexion*. In the two poems on Platonic Love we may alfo difcern the prefence of the mafter. It would, of courfe, be abfurd to affert that the lyric poetry of Donne had no influence on that of Herbert, but its influence was far lefs confiderable than it would at firft fight appear to be. Herbert's rhythm is his own. Where it is mufical its mufic is not the mufic of the older poet, where its note is harfh and diffonant it is no echo of the difcords of that unequal and moft capricious finger. Many of Donne's favourite meafures he has not employed; fome of his own meafures, the meafures in which he has been moft fuccefsful, have no prototype in Donne's poems. What he owes in lyric poetry to the leader of the Metaphyfical School is to be found, fo far as form is concerned, rather in what Donne fuggefted than in what he directly taught. In fpirit he owed, it muft be allowed, much. From Donne he learned to fport with extravagant fancies, to substitute the language of the schools for the language of the heart, to think like the author of the *Enneads* and to write like the author of *Euphues.* He has, however, had the good taste to avoid the grosser faults of his master. He never indulges in preposterous absurdities; he never, if we except one couplet, clothes mysticism in motley.

Herbert's poems are of too miscellaneous a character to be exactly classified. They may be roughly divided into Sonnets, Elegies, Epitaphs, Satires, Miscellaneous Lyrics, and Occasional Pieces. However unequal these compositions may be in point of execution, there are two things which the reader of Herbert may, in the more ambitious poems at least, generally promise himself—originality and vigour. The Sonnets need not detain us long. The one 'To his Watch' (page 1) is well expressed. The style is in happy unison with the sentiment, and the final clause is solemn and impressive. The last verse of the sonnet ' To her Face ' (page 6),

'Sure Adam sinn'd not in that spotless face,'

though somewhat obscure, is a really fine line. In the sonnet written near Merlou Castle (page 12), the couplet describing the groves on the banks of the stream,

' Embroidering through each glade
An airy silver and a sunny gold,'

prove that Herbert had the eye of a poet. The moſt ſtriking of them is the addreſs 'To Black Itſelf' (page 59), which is particularly intereſting, becauſe it contains the germ of part at leaſt of the idea which was afterwards ſo magnificently embodied by Blanco White in his famous ſonnet. White was moſt likely immediately indebted to Sir Thomas Browne, but Browne **was no** doubt well acquainted with Herbert and his writings. With regard to his Elegies—I am not, of courſe, including among them the lyric elegy on page 49—I ſhall perhaps conſult his fame beſt by paſſing them by without comment. Two or three verſes in the ' Elegy on the Prince ' will no doubt pleaſe and ſtrike, but there praiſe muſt end, even from an editor. Of the Epitaphs, the moſt original is the ' Epitaph upon Himſelf' (page 81), the moſt grotefque that on Cecilia Boulfer (page 29), the **moſt** eloquent and pleaſing that on William Herbert of **Swanſey** (page **31**). The two ſatires are of **very** unequal merit. The ſecond, page **20**, would diſgrace Taylor the Water Poet. The firſt, ' The State Progreſs of Ill,' though intolerably harſh and barbarous in ſtyle, contains ſome intereſting remarks. Of the Occaſional Pieces, thoſe which moſt nearly reſembled the poems of which we have been ſpeaking are the verſes entitled ' To her Mind ' (page 8), and ' To his Miſtreſs for her True Picture' (page 74), both being in the heroic couplet, and both being in the ſame contemplative vein. To thofe who are fond of tracing refemblances between the works of men of genius who are feparated by many years from each other, it will be interefting to obferve how clofely Herbert fometimes reminds us of Mr. Browning. In the verfes, for example, 'To her Mind,' there is a paffage which might excufably be miftaken for the work of the great philofophical poet of our day :—

> 'Thus ends my Love, but this doth grieve me moft
> That fo it ends ; but that ends too ; this yet,
> Befide the wifhes, hopes and time I loft,
> Troubles my mind awhile, that I am fet
> Free, worfe than deny'd : I can neither boaft
> Choice nor fuccefs, as my cafe is, nor get
> Pardon from myfelf, that I loved not
> A better miftrefs, or her worfe. This debt
> Only 's her due, ftill that fhe be forgot
> Ere chang'd, left I love none ; this done, the taint
> Of foul inconftancy is cleared at leaft
> In me ; there only refts but to unpaint
> Her form in my mind, that fo difpoffeff'd,
> It be a temple, but without a faint.'

—the fame elliptical mode of expreffion, the fame intermixture of fentiment and logic, the fame curious refinements of fpeculative meditation. The verfes 'To his Miftrefs for her True Picture' will not find, and they certainly do not deferve, many admirers. It may be queftioned whether Platonifm **has** ever clothed itfelf in fuch grotefque language as in **the** laft couplet of this ftrange poem :

> ' Hear from my body's prifon this my call,
>   Who from my mouth-grate and eye-window bawl.'

The lyric pieces are of very unequal merit. But in making out a cafe for Herbert **my** bufinefs is only with his beft work ; and if we judge him by his beft work, **he** is certainly entitled to no mean place among the lyrifts of the Metaphyfical School. His mufic is, it muft **be** owned, full of difcords—his verfes will fometimes not even fcan, and yet he poffeffed not only **a** fine ear for rhythmic effect, but his rhythm is of great compafs and variety. Occafionally **his** verfe **has a** weight, a fullnefs and dignity, not unworthy of Dryden ; for example, **two** ftanzas like thefe (pages 10 and **11**) :

> ' Nay, thou art greater, **too !** More deftiny
>   Depends on thee than on her influence.
>   No hair thy fatal hand doth now difpenfe
> But to fome one a thread of life muft be.

> *   *   *   *   *

> ' But ftay ! methinks new beauties do arife
>   While fhe withdraws thefe glories which were fpread.
>   Wonder of Beauties ! fet thy radiant head,
> And ftrike out Day from thy yet fairer eyes.'

Nor can we refuſe the gift of lyric melody to the writer of a ſtanza like this :—

> ‘ Then think each minute that you loſe a day.
>   The longeſt youth is ſhort,
>   The ſhorteſt age is long : Time flies away,
>   And makes us but his ſport,
>   And that which is not Youth’s is Age’s prey.’

Or to the writer of ſuch poems as we find on page 56, and on page 46.

But Herbert’s greateſt metrical triumph is that he was the firſt to diſcover the harmony of that ſtanza with which the moſt celebrated poet of our own day has familiariſed us. The glory of having invented it belongs indeed to another, but the glory of having paſſed it almoſt perfect into Mr. Tennyſon’s hands belongs unqueſtion-ably to Herbert. And it is due alſo to Herbert to ſay that he not only revealed its ſweetneſs and beauty, but that he anticipated ſome of its moſt exquiſite effects and variations. Take, for example, the following ſtanza, where the pauſe occurs at the end of the ſecond line :—

> ‘ For where affection once is ſhown,
>   No longer can the World beguile ;
>   Who ſees his penance all the while
>   He holds a torch to make her known.’—*Ditty*, page 42.

Or thefe lines, where the paufe is made at the end of the
firft line :—

> ' Elfe fhould our fouls in vain elect,
>> And vainer yet were Heaven's laws
>> When to an everlafting caufe
>> They give a perifhing effect.'—Page 96.

Or again :—

> ' Nay, I proteft ; though Death with his
>> Worft counfel fhould divide us here ;'—Page **94.**

where the paufe occurs at **the end of** the fourth fyllable.
An analytical examination of the metre of *In Memoriam*
will fhow that on alternations and interchanges of thofe
paufes the poet has not only relied for varying his harmony, but for producing fome of his moft pleafing effects.
Indeed, in Herbert's two poems we find anticipated the
exact cadence, the exact note of the modern poet. I
queftion, for example, whether the niceft ear **could dis-**
tinguifh lines like thefe from the Laureate's :—

> ' Were not our fouls immortal made,
>> Our equal loves can make them fuch.'

> ' As one another's myftery,
>> Each fhall be both, yet both but one.'

> ' Who fees his penance all the while
>> He holds a torch to make her known.'

Other points of refemblance, into which there is no

neceffity for entering here, can fcarcely fail to fuggeft themfelves to thoughtful readers. It is curious that we fhould be able to point—and to point, I venture to think, without at all ftraining analogy—to two poems of this forgotten poet which recall fo exactly the work of the author of *In Memoriam* and the work of the author of *Sordello.* If the circumftance prove little elfe, it proves at leaft the verfatility of Herbert's powers.

The beft of Herbert's lyrics is the poem of which we have juft been fpeaking — the 'Ode upon a Queftion moved whether Love fhould Continue for Ever.' It is a little prolix, and it is occafionally obfcure; but the fineft ftanzas in it are exquifitely beautiful. Next would come, in the eftimation of many perhaps, the verfes 'Upon combing her Hair' (page 10), which are fingularly vigorous and picturefque. We feel, however, that their founding rhetoric is fomewhat out of place—the ftyle is too elevated for the theme, a common fault with poets of the fecond order. Among other lyrics of a ferious caft the 'Elegy over a Tomb' (page 49) and the verfes 'To her Hair' (page 56) deferve mention. Of the lighter lyrics the 'Ditty in Imitation of the Spanifh' will probably be read with much pleafure. The Platonic Love poems, though not without intereft and even merit, cannot be faid to hold a very high rank among poems of the clafs to which they belong. With one exception—the ode on page 92, to which I have already referred—they are little calculated either to pleafe or to ftrike. They have all the frigidity and pedantic ingenuity of Petrarch and Bembo without thofe beauties of expreffion which ftill attract us in the Sonnetti and Canzoni. 'The Idea' is, however, well worth attentive perufal. Rarely have the doctrines of pure Platonifm been more fkilfully applied, rarely have philofophy and fentiment been more ingenioufly blended.

Herbert's moft confpicuous defects, both in thefe and in his other poems, are want of finifh and exceffive obfcurity. He feldom does juftice to his conceptions. He had evidently no love for the labour of the file, and he has paid, like Donne and Fulke Greville, the juft penalty for his careleffnefs.

The Latin poems of Herbert are fcarcely likely to find favour in the eyes of modern fcholars. Their diction is, as a rule, involved and obfcure; they teem with forced and unclaffical expreffions. His hendecafyllabics are intolerably harfh, and violate almoft every metrical canon. His Elegiacs are not more fuccefsful; indeed, the only tolerable copy among the poemata are the verfes on a Dial, for the epigrams are below contempt. In his hexameters he fucceeds better. The 'Menfa Luforia' is ingenious and not inelegant, and the 'Pro Laureato Poetâ,' though unneceffarily obfcure, is, like the epiftle to Guftavus, extremely fpirited. But even at his beft he

cannot for an inftant be compared with his contemporaries, Owen, Milton, Cowley, or May, who wrote
Latin, nor indeed with the purity of the poets of the
Italian Renaiffance, but with wonderful fluency and
vigour. Befide the Latin poems appearing in this volume,
Herbert was the author of three others, entitled refpec-
tively 'Hæredibus ac Nepotibus fuis Præcepta,' which is in
elegiacs, ' De Vitâ Humanâ Philofophica Difquifitio,' and
' De Vitâ Cœlefti ex ejufdem principiis Conjeϵtura,' which
are in hexameters. They are to be found among certain
traϵts appended to the *De Caufis Errorum*, printed in
1645.* The two laft appear alfo in the *Autobiography*,
and they are by far the beft. But as thefe poems are not
likely to intereft readers in our day, and poffefs little or
no value in themfelves, we have refrained from adding
them, even by way of appendix, to the prefent volume.

---

* The exaϵt title of the volume is, *De Caufis Errorum, una
cum traϵtatu De Religione Laici et Appendice ad Sacerdotes, necnon
quibufdam poematibus. Londini*, 1645 (Walpole fays, erroneoufly,
1647).

OCCASIONAL
VERSES

OF

EDWARD LORD HERBERT

BARON

OF

CHERBURY AND CASTLE-ISLAND.

Deceased in August 1648.

LONDON:

Printed by T. R. *for* THOMAS DRING,

At THE GEORGE *in* FLEET STREET, *near* CLIFFORD'S INN.

1665.

To the

RIGHT HON. EDWARD LORD HERBERT,

BARON OF CHERBERY IN ENGLAND AND

CASTLE ISLAND IN IRELAND.

My Lord,

 This Collection of some of the scattered Copies of Verses, composed in various and perplexed times, by Edward Lord Herbert, your late Grandfather, belongs of double right to your Lordship, as Heir and Executor ; and had it been in his power to have bequeathed his Learning by Will, as his Library and Personal Estate, it may be presumed he would have given it to you as the best Legacy. But Learning being not of our Gift, though of our Acquisition, nor of the Parapharnalia of a Lady's Chamber, nor of the casual and fortunate Goods of the World, it must be acknowledged of a transcendency beyond natural things, and a beam of the Divinity. For by the Powers of Knowledge **Men** are not only diſtinguiſhed from **Men,** but carried above **the** reach **of ordinary** Perſons, to give Reaſons even of their Belief——not that men believe becauſe they know, but know becauſe **they** believe. Faith muſt precede Knowledge ; and yet men are not bound to accept matters of Religion, though Religion be the objeɛt and employment of faith, not of reaſoning merely without Reaſon and probable Inducements.

That the learned Centuries are paſt, and **Learning** in declenſion, is **too** great a truth, which may **in**troduce Atheiſme with Ignorance ; for as Ignorance is the Mother of Devotion amongſt the Papiſts, ſo 'tis the Mother of Atheiſme amongſt the Ignorant.

The great and moſt dangerous deſign of our Church and National Enemies, **is** to make us **out** of Love with Learning, as **a** Mechanick thing **and** beneath the Spirits of the Nobility and of Princes : whereas nothing improves and enlightens **the** underſtandings of great Perſons but Learning, and not only ennobles them far above their birth, but enables them to impoſe on others, and to give rather than take advice. The Learned, Generous, and Vertuous Perſon needs no

Anceſtors. And what can ſo properly be call'd ours as what is of our purchaſe?

'Gentiles agunt ſub nomine Chriſtiano' *was an old Reproach upon the Primitive Chriſtians; and* now **Men** *out-aEt* **the** *Gentiles.*

The Goods of this life are all Hydropick, Quo plus bibuntur, plus ſitiuntur.   *Men* **are** *the* **drier** *for drinking and the poorer for covetouſneſs: no ſatiety, no fulneſs, but in ſpiritual things. The way of Vertue appeared to the Heathen to* **be** *the only way to Happineſs, and yet they knew* not *many vertues which* **are the** *Glory of Chriſtianity, as Humility, Denying of our ſelves, Taking up the Croſs, for-giving* **and** *loving our Enemies, which* **the** *Heathen took for follies rather* **than** *Vertues.*

As for Poetry, it bears date before Proſe, **and** *was of ſo great authority with the common People and the wiſer ſort of antiquity, that* it *was* **in** *veneration with* **their** *Sacred* **Writ** *and Records, from which* **they** **derived** *their divinity and belief concerning their Gods,* **and** *that their Poets,* **as** *Orpheus, Linus,* **and** *Muſæus, were deſcended of the Gods, and divinely inſpired, from the* **extra-**

ordinary Motions of their Minds, **and** from the Relations of ſtrange Viſions, **Raptures,** and Apparitions.

My Lord, **excuſe the** liberty of this Dedication, **and** believe **me,**

Your Lordſhip's Uncle

and Humble Servant,

HENRY HERBERT.

March 18th, 166⅘.

OCCASIONAL VERSES.

TO HIS WATCH

WHEN HE COULD NOT SLEEP.

UNCESSANT Minutes, whilſt you move you tell
   The time that tells our life, which, though it run
  Never ſo faſt or far, your new begun
Short ſteps ſhall overtake ; for though life well

May ſcape his own Account, it ſhall not yours.
   You are Death's Auditors, that both divide
  And ſum what ere that life inſpir'd endures
   Paſt a beginning, and through you we bide

The doom of Fate, whoſe unrecall'd Decree
   You date, bring, execute ; making what's new
   Ill, and good old, for as we die in you,
You die in Time, Time in Eternity.

B

DITTY.

D EEP Sighs, Records of my unpitied Grief,
 　　Memorials of my true though hopeleſs Love,
Keep time with my ſad thoughts, till wiſh'd Relief
My long deſpairs for vain and cauſleſs prove.
Yet if ſuch hap never to you befall,
I give you leave, break time, break heart, and all.

Lord, thus I ſin, repent, and ſin again,
As if Repentance only were in me
Leave for new Sin ; thus do I entertain
My ſhort time, and Thy Grace, abuſing Thee
And Thy long ſuffering, which, though it be
Ne'er overcome by Sin, yet were in vain
If tempted oft : thus we our Errors ſee

Before our Puniſhment, and ſo remain
Without Excuſe : and, Lord, in them 'tis true
Thy Laws are juſt ; but why doſt Thou diſtrain
Ought elſe for life ſave life ?　That is Thy due,
The reſt Thou mak'ſt us owe, and may'ſt to us
As well forgive.　But, oh ! my ſins renew,
Whilſt I do talk with my Creator thus.

2

A DESCRIPTION.

*I SING her worth and praifes, I,
 Of whom a Poet cannot lie.
The little World the **Great fhall** blaze,
Sea, Earth, her Body; **Heaven, her Face,**
Her Hair, Sunbeams, whofe every part
Lightens, inflames **each Lover's Heart,**
That thus you prove the **†Axiom true,**
Whilft the Sun helped Nature **in you.**
Her Front, the white and **azure** fky
In Light and Glory raifed high,
Being o'recaft **by a cloudy** frown,
All Hearts **and Eyes** dejecteth **down ;**
Her each **Brow, a celeftial Bow**
Which through this Sky **her** Light doth fhow,
Which doubled, if it ftrange appear
The Sun's likewife is doubled there ;
Her either Cheek, a blufhing Morn,
Which, on the Wings **of Beauty** born,
Doth never fet, but only **fair**
Shineth exalted in her hair ;

---

* μικρόκοσμος μακροκόσμος.   † *Sol et homo generant hominem.*

Within her Mouth Heaven's Heav'n reside ;
Her words the souls there Glorifi'd ;
Her Nose, th'Æquator of this Globe,
Where Nakedness, Beauty's best Robe,
Presents a form all Hearts to win.
Last Nature made that Dainty Chin,
Which that it might in every fashion
Answer the rest, a Constellation
Like to a Desk, She there did place
To write the Wonders of her Face.
In this Cœlestial Frontispiece,
Where Happiness eternal lies,
First arranged stand three Senses,—
This Heaven's Intelligences,
Whose several Motions sweet combined
Come from the first Mover, her Mind.
The weight of this Harmonique Sphere
The Atlas of her Neck doth bear,
Whose favours Day to Us imparts
When Frowns make Night in Lovers' Hearts.
Two foaming Billows are her Breasts,
That carry rais'd upon their Crests
The Tyrian Fish : More white's their Foam
Then that whence Venus once did come.
Here take her by the Hand, my Muse,
With that Sweet Foe, to make my Truce,

To compact Manna beft compar'd,
Whofe dewy infide's not full hard.
Her Waift's an enverf'd Pyramis
Upon whofe Cone Love's Trophy is.
Her Belly is that Magazine
At whofe peep Nature did refigne
That precious Mould by which alone
There can be framed fuch a One :
At th' entrance of which hidden Treafure,
Happy making above meaffure,
Two Alabafter Pillars ftand,
To warn all paffage from that Land,
At foot whereof engraved is
The fad *Non Ultra* of Man's Blifs.
The back of this moft pretious Frame
Holds up in Majefty the Same ;
Where to make Mufic to all Hearts
Love bound the defcant of her parts.
Though all this Beauty's Temple be
There's known within no Deity
Save Virtues fhrin'd within her Will.
As I began, fo fay I ftill,
I fing her Worth and Praifes, I,
Of whom a Poet cannot lie.

TO HER FACE.

FATAL Afpect! that haft an *influence*
  More powerful far than thofe Immortal Fires
That but incline the Will and move the Senfe
Which thou alone conftrainft, kindling defires
Of fuch a holy force, as more infpires
The Soul with Knowledge, than Experience
Or Revelation can do with all
Their borrow'd helps : Sacred Aftonifhment
Sits on thy Brow, threat'ning a fudden fall
To all thofe Thoughts that are not lowly fent
In wonder and amaze, dazzling that Eye
Which on thofe Myfteries doth rudely gaze.
Vow'd only unto Love's Divinity :
Sure Adam finn'd not in that fpotlefs Face.

TO HER BODY.

REGARDFUL Prefence! whofe fix'd Majefty
　　Darts Admiration on the gazing Look
That brings it not : State fits enthron'd in thee,
Divulging forth her Laws in the fair Book
Of thy Commandëments, which none miftook
That ever humbly came therein to fee
Their own unworthinefs.　Oh, how can I
Enough admire that Symmetry, expreft
In new Proportions, which doth give the Lie
To that Arithmetic which hath profeft
All Numbers to be Hers?　Thy Harmony
Comes from the Spheres, and there doth prove
Strange meafures, fo well grac'd, as Majefty
Itfelf like thee would reft, like thee would move.

TO HER MIND.

EXALTED Mind! Whofe character doth bear
　　The firft idea of Perfection, whence
Adam's came, and ftands fo.　How can'ft appear
In words that only tell **what here-**
Tofore hath been?　Thou need'ft as deep a fenfe
As Prophecy, fince there's no difference
In telling what thou art and what fhalt be.
Then pardon me that Rapture do profefs
At thy outfide, that want for what I fee
Defcription of.　Here amaz'd I ceafe
Thus——
Yet grant one queftion and no more, crav'd **under**
Thy gracious leave :　**How, if thou** wouldft exprefs
Thyfelf **to us, thou** fhouldft be ftill a wonder?

Thus ends my Love, but this doth grieve me moft
That fo it ends ; but that ends too ; this yet,
Befides the Wifhes, hopes, and time I loft,
Troubles my mind awhile, **that I am fet**

8

To her Mind.

Free, worſe than denied : I can neither boaſt
Choice nor Succeſs as my Caſe is, nor get
Pardon from myſelf, that I loved not
A better Miſtreſs, or her worſe.   This Debt
Only's her due, ſtill that ſhe be forgot
Ere chang'd, left I love none : this done, the taint
Of foul Inconſtancy is clear'd at leaſt.
In me, there only reſts but to unpaint
Her form in my mind, that ſo diſpoſſeſt,
It be a Temple, but without a Saint.

UPON COMBING HER HAIR.

BREAKING from under that thy cloudy Veil
  Open and fhine yet more ; fhine out more clear,
Thou glorious golden-beam-darting hair,
Even till my wonder-ftricken Senfes fail.

Shoot out in light, and fhine thofe Rays on far,
Thou much more fair than is the Queen of Love,
When fhe doth comb her in her Sphere above,
And from a Planet turns a Blazing Star.

Nay, thou art greater, too !   More deftiny
Depends on thee than on her influence.
No hair thy fatal hand doth now difpenfe,
But to fome one a thred of life muft be.

While gracious unto me thou both doft funder
Thofe glories which, if they united were,
Might have amazed fenfe, and fhew'ft each hair
Which, if alone, had been too great a wonder.

And now fpread in their goodly length, fh'appears
No creature which the earth might call her own;
But rather one that, in her gliding down,
Heav'ns beams did crown, to fhew us fhe was theirs.

And come from thence, how can they fear Time's rage,
Which in his power elfe on earth moft ftrange,
Such golden treafure doth to Silver change
By that improper Alchemy of Age?

But ftay! methinks new Beauties do arife
While fhe withdraws thefe Glories which were fpread:
Wonder of Beauties! fet thy radiant head,
And ftrike out Day from thy yet fairer eyes.

DITTY IN IMITATION OF THE SPANISH
ENTRE TANTOQUE EL'AVRIL.

NOW that the April of your youth adorns
  The garden of your face,
Now that for you each knowing Lover mourns,
  And all feek to your grace,
Do not repay affection with fcorns.

What though you may a matchlefs Beauty vaunt,
  And all that Hearts can move
By such a power that feemeth to enchant,
  Yet, without help of Love,
Beauty no pleafure to itfelf can grant.

Then think each minute that you lofe a day.
  The longeft youth is fhort,
The fhorteft Age is long; Time flies away,
  And makes us but his fport,
And that which is not Youth's is Age's prey.

12

See but the braveſt Horſe that prideth moſt,
　　Though he eſcaped the War,
Either from Maſter to the Man, is loſt,
　　Or turned unto the Car;
Or elſe muſt die with being ridden Poſt.

Then loſe not Beauty, Lovers, Time, and all,
　　Too late your fault you ſee,
When that in vain you would theſe days recall.
　　Nor can you virtuous be,
When without theſe you have not wherewithal.

THE STATE-PROGRESS OF ILL.

I SAY, 'tis hard to write Satires.   Though Ill
 Great'ned in his long courfe, and fwelling ftill,
Be now like to a Deluge, yet, as Nile,
'Tis doubtful in his original.   This while
We may thus much on either part prefume,
That what fo univerfal are, muft come
From caufes great and far.   Now in this State
Of things, which is leaft like good, Men hate,
Since 'twill be the lefs fin.   I do fee
Some ill required, that one poifon might free
The other; fo ftates, to their Greatnefs, find
No faults required but their own, and bind
The reft.   And though this be myfterious, ftill,
Why fhould we not imagine how this Ill
Did come at firft, how't keeps his greatnefs here,
When 'tis difguif'd, and when it doth appear.
This Ill, having fome attributes of God
As to have made it felf and bear the rod
Of all our punifhments, as it feems, came

Into the World to rule it, and to tame
The pride of Goodnefs ; and though his Reign
Great in the hearts of men he doth maintain
By love, not right, he yet the tyrant here
(Though it be him we love and God we fear),
Pretence yet wants not, that it was before
Some part of Godhead, **as Mercy,** that ftore
For Souls grown Bankrupt, their firft ftock of Grace,
And that which the finner of the laft **place**
Shall number out, unlefs th' Higheft will **fhow**
Some power not yet reveal'd to Man below.

But that I may proceed, and fo go on
To trace Ill in his firft progreffion,
And through his Secret'ft ways, and where that he
Had left his nakednefs as well as we,
And did appear himfelf,

   I note that in $\left\{ \begin{array}{c} \text{Gradus} \\ \text{mali funt} \\ \text{quo.} \end{array} \right\}$ Peccamus **nobis.**
The yet infant world how
   Mifchief and fin,   Nocemus aliis.
His Agents here on earth, and eafy known,
Are now concealed Intelligencers grown :
For fince that as a Guard th' Higheft at once
Put Fear t' attend their private actions,
And Shame their publick, other means being fail'd,
Mifchief under doing of Good was veil'd,

And Sin, of Pleasure; though in this disguise
They only hide themselves from mortal eyes.
Sins, those that both com- and o-mitted be,
Once hot and cold, but in a third degree
Are now such poisons, that though they may lurk
In secret parts awhile, yet they will work
Though after death; nor ever come alone,
But sudden-fruitful multiply ere done.
While in this monstrous birth they only die
Whom we confess, those live which we deny.
Mischiefs, like fatal Constellations,
Appear unto the ignorant at once
In glory and in hurt, while th'unseen part
Of the great cause may be perchance the Art
Of th' Ill and hiding it, which that I may
Ev'n in his first original display,
And best example, sure amongst Kings, he,
Who first wanted successions to be,
A Tyrant was, wise enough to have chose
An honest man for King, which should dispose
Those beasts, which being so tame, yet otherwise
As it seems, could not herd; And with advise
Somewhat indifferent for both, he might
Yet have provided for their Children's right,
If they grew wiser, not his own, that so
They might repent, yet under treason, who

Ne'er promis'd faith : though now we cannot spare
(And not be worse) Kings, on those terms, they are
No worse than we could spare (and have been sav'd)
Original sin. So then those Priests that rav'd
And prophesy'd, they did a kind of good
They knew not of, by whom the choice first stood.
   Since, then, we may consider now as fit
State government, and all the Acts of it,
That we may know them yet, let us see how
They were derived, done, and are maintained now,
That Princes may by this yet understand
Why we obey as well as they command.
State a proportion'd colour'd table is,
Nobility the master-piece in this,
Serves to shew distances ; while being put
'Twixt sight and vastness they seem higher, but
As they're further off ; yet as those blue hills
Which th'utmost border of a Region fills,
They are great and worse parts, while in the steep
Of this great Prospective they seem to keep
Further absent from those below, though this
Exalted Spirit, that's sure a free Soul, is
A greater Privilege than to be born
At Venice, although he seek not rule, doth scorn
Subjection, but as he is flesh, and so
He is to dulness, shame, and **many moe**

Such properties, knows, but the Painter's Art,
All in the frame is equal.   That deſert
Is a more living thing, and doth obey
As he gives poor, for God's ſake (though they
And Kings aſk it not ſo), thinks Honours are
Figures compoſ'd of lines irregular,
And happy-high knows no election
Raiſeth man to true Greatneſs but his own.
Meanwhile ſugar'd Divines, next place to this,
Tell us Humility and Patience is
The way to Heaven, and that we muſt there
Look for our Kingdom ; that the great'ſt rule here
Is for to rule ourſelves.   And that they might
Say this the better, they to no place have right
B'inheritance, while whom Ambition ſways,
Their office is to turn it other ways.
   Thoſe yet, whoſe harder minds Religion
Cannot invade, nor turn from thinking on
A preſent greatneſs, that combin'd curſe of Law
Of officers' and Neighbours' ſpite doth draw
Within ſuch whirlpools, that till they be drown'd
They ne'er get out, but only ſwim them round.
   Thus brief, ſince that the infinite of ill
Is neither eaſie told nor ſafe, I will
But only note how freeborn Man, ſubdu'd
By his own choice, that was at firſt endu'd

With equal power over all, doth now ſubmit
That infinite of Number, Spirit, Wit,
To ſome eight Monarchs.   Then why wonder Men
      Their rule of horſes ?
The world, as in the Ark of Noah, reſts
Compoſ'd as then, few Men and many Beaſts.

Aug. 1608.
At Merlou in **France.**

SATYRA SECUNDA

OF TRAVELLERS FROM PARIS.

BEN JOHNSON, travel is a ſecond birth
    Unto the Children of another Earth ;
Only as our King Richard was, ſo they appear,
New born to another World, with teeth and hair.
While got by Engliſh Parents, carried in
Some Womb of thirty-tun and lightly twin,
They are delivered at Calais or at Dieppe,
And ſtrangely ſtand, go feed themſelves, nay, keep
Their own money ſtreightways ; but that is all,
For none can underſtand them when they call
For anything. No more than Badger,
That call'd the Queen Monſieur, laid a wager
With the King of his Dogs who underſtood
Them all alike, which Badger thought was good.
But that I may proceed. Since their birth is
Only a kind of Metempſychoſis,
Such Knowledge as their Memory could give
They have for help, what time theſe Souls do live
In Engliſh clothes ; a body which again

They never rife unto, but, as you fee
When they come home, like children yet that be
Of their own bringing up ; all they learn is
Toys and the Language, but to attain this
You muft conceive they're cofen'd, mocked, and come
To Fourbourgs St. Germans, there take a Room
Lightly about th' Ambaffadors, and where,
Having no Church, they come Sundays to hear
An invitation which they have moft part,
If their outfide but promife a defert,
To fit above the Secretaries' place,
Although it be almoft as rare a cafe
To fee Englifh well cloth'd here, as with you
At London, Indians.   But that your view
May comprehend at once them gone for Blois
Or Orleans ; learn'd French, now no more Boys
But perfect men at Paris, putting on
Some forc'd difguife, or labour'd fafhion,
To appear ftrange at home, befides their ftay,
Laugh and look on with me, to fee what they
Are now become ; but that the poorer fort,
A fubject not fit for my Mufe nor fport,
May pafs untouch'd, let's but confider what
Elpus is now become, once young, handfome, and that
Was fuch a Wit, as very well with four
Of the fix might have made one, and no more,

Had he been at their Valentine, and could
Agree, your Rus fhould ufe the ftock who would
Carefully in that, ev'n as 'twere his own
Put out their Jefts, briefly one that was grown
Ripe to another tafte than that wherein
He is now feafoned and dry'd, as in
His face by this you fee, which would perplex
A ftranger to define his years, or fex ;
To which his wrinkles, when he fpeaks doth give
That Age his words fhould have, while he doth ftrive,
As if fuch births had never come from brain
To fhew his mots deliver'd without pain,
Nor without After-throes.   Sometimes as grace
Did overflow in circles o're his face,
Ev'n to the brim, which he thinks fure
If this pofture do but fo long endure
That it be fix'd by Age he'll look as like
A fpeaking fign, as our St. George to ftrike,
That, where he is, none but will hold their peace
If th' have but the leaft good manners, or confefs,
If he fhould fpeak, he did prefume **too far**
In fpeaking then, when others readier are.
Now that he fpeaks are complemental fpeeches
That never go off but below the breeches
Of him he doth falute, while he doth wring
And with fome loofe French words which **he** doth
    ftring,   **22**

Windeth about **the arms, the** legs **and** ſides,
Moſt ſerpent-like of any man that **bides**
His indirect approach, which being done
Almoſt without an introduction,
If he have heard but any bragging French
Boaſt of the favor of ſome noble wench,
He'll ſwear 'twas he did her graces poſſeſs,
And damn his own ſoul **for** the wickedneſs
Of other men, ſtrangeſt of all **in** that.
But I am weary to deſcribe you what,
Ere this, you can.   As for the little **fry**
That all along the ſtreet turn up the eye
At everything they meet, that have not yet
Seen that ſwol'n vicious Queen Margaret,
Who were a monſter ev'n without her ſin,
Nor the Italian comedies wherein
Women play Boys.——I ceaſe to write.
To end this Satire and bid thee good **Night**.

Sept. 1608.

23

I MUST depart, but like to his laſt breath
    That leaves the ſeat of life for liberty,
I go, but dying, and in this our death
Where ſoul and ſoul is parted, it is I
      The deader part yet fly away,
        While ſhe, alas ! in whom before
        I liv'd, dies her own death and more,
      I feeling mine too much, and her own ſtay.
But ſince I muſt depart, and that our love
Springing at firſt but in an earthly mould
Tranſplanted to our ſouls, now doth remove
Earthly affects, which time and diſtance would,
      Nothing now can our loves allay,
        Though as the better Spirits will
        That both love us and know our ill,
      We do not either all the good we may.
Thus when our Souls that muſt immortal be,
    For our loves cannot die, nor we (unleſs
We die not both together) ſhall be free
    Unto their open and eternal peace.
Sleep, Death's Embaſſador, and beſt
    Image, doth yours often ſo ſhow,
    That I thereby muſt plainly know,
Death unto us muſt be freedom and reſt.

May 1608.

MADRIGAL.

HOW should I love my best?
    What though my love unto that height be grown,
        That taking joy in you alone,
      I utterly this world detest.
Should I not love it **yet** as th' only place,
    Where Beauty hath his perfect grace,
      And is posfest?

      But I beauties despise.
You, universal beauty seem to me,
    Giving and shewing form and degree
      To all the rest, in your fair eyes.
Yet should I not love them as parts whereon
    Your beauty, their perfection,
      And top doth rise?

      But ev'n my self I **hate**.
So far my love is from the least delight,
    That at my very self I spite.
      Senseless of any happy state,
Yet may I not with justest reason fear,
    How hating hers, I **truly** her
      Can **celebrate**?

Madrigal.

Thus unresolved still,
Although world, life, nay what is fair beside,
I cannot for your sake abide,
Methinks I love not to my fill.
Yet, if a greater love you can devise,
In loving you some otherwise,
Believe't I will.

ANOTHER.

D EAR, when I did from you remove,
    I left my joy, but not my love;
      That never can depart.
It neither higher can afcend,
    Nor lower bend.
Fixt in the centre of my heart,
    As in his place,
And lodged fo, how can it change,
    Or you grow ftrange?
Thofe are earth's properties and bafe.
Each where, as the bodies divine,
    Heav'n's lights and you to me will fhine.

TO HIS FRIEND BEN JOHNSON, OF HIS HORACE MADE ENGLISH.

IT was not enough Ben Johnſon to be thought
  Of Engliſh Poets beſt, but to have brought
In greater ſtate to their acquaintance one
So equal to himſelf and thee, that none
Might be thy ſecond, while thy Glory is
To be the Horace of our times and his.

EPITAPH. CÆCIL-BOULFER

QUÆ POST LANGUESCENTEM MORBUM
NON SINE INQUIETUDINE
SPIRITUS &c. CONSCIENTIÆ OBIIT.

Intelligitur
de figurâ
mortis
præfigendâ.

METHINKS Death like one laughing lies,
 Shewing his teeth, fhutting his eyes,
Only thus to have found her here
He did with fo much reafon fear,
 And fhe defpife.

For barring all the gates of Sin,
Death's open ways to enter in,
She was with a ftrict fiege befet,
So what by force he could not get,
 By time to win.

This mighty Warrior was deceived yet,
For what he mutin * in her powers, thought
 Was but their zeal ;
And what by their excefs might have been wrought,
 Her fafts did heal.

---

* Mutiny.

29

Till that her noble foul, by thefe, as wings,
Tranfcending **the low pitch of** earthly things,
As being reliev'd **by God and fet at** large,
And grown by this, worthy a higher charge,
Triumphing over Death to Heaven fled,
And did not die, but left her body dead.

July 1609.

EPITAPH. GULI. HERBERT DE SWANSEY
QUI SINE PROLE OBIIT AUG. 1609.

GREAT Spirit, that in New Ambition,
    Stoop'd not below his merit,
But with his proper worth being carry'd on,
Stoop'd at no fecond place, till now in one
    He doth all place inherit.

Live endlefs here in fuch brave memory,
    The beft tongue cannot fpot it;
While they which knew, or but have heard of thee,
Muft never hope thy like again to be,
    Since thou haft not begot it.

IN A GLASS WINDOW FOR INCONSTANCY.

L OVE, of this cleareſt, fraileſt glaſs,
    Divide the properties, ſo as
In the diviſion may appear
Clearneſs for me, frailty for her.

ELEGY FOR THE PRINCE.*

MUST he be ever dead? Cannot we add
    Another life unto that Prince that had
Our ſouls laid up in him? Could not our love,
Now when he left us, make that body move
After his death one Age? And keep unite
That frame wherein our ſouls did ſo delight?
For what are ſouls but love? ſince they do know
Only for it, and can no further go.
Senſe is the Soul of Beaſts, becauſe none can
Proceed ſo far as t'underſtand like man.
And if Souls be more where they love than where
They animate, why did it not appear
In keeping him alive? Or how is fate
Equal to us, when one man's private hate
May ruin Kingdoms, when he will expoſe
Himſelf to certain death, and yet all thoſe
Not keep alive this Prince, who now is gone,
Whoſe loves would give thouſands of lives for one?,
Do we then die in him, only as we
May in the world's harmonique body ſee
An univerſally diffuſed ſoul

---

* Henry, Prince of Wales. He died in November, 1612.

D

Elegy for the Prince.

Move in the parts which moves not in the whole?
So though **we** reft with him, we do appear
To live and ftir awhile, **as** if he were
Still quickening us? Or do (perchance) we live
And know it not? **See** we not Autumn give
Back to the earth again what it received
In th' early Spring? And may not we deceived
Think that thofe powers are dead, which do but fleep,
And the world's foul doth reunited keep?
And though this Autumn gave what never more
Any Spring can unto the world reftore,
May **we** not **be** deceived, and think we know
Ourfelves for **dead**? Becaufe that we are fo
Unto each other, when as yet we **live**
A life his **love** and memory doth give,
Who was our world's foul, and to whom we are
So reunite, that in him we repair
All other our affections ill beftowed:
Since **by** this love we now have fuch abode
With him in Heaven **as we** had here, before
He left us dead. **N**or fhall we queftion more
Whether the Soul of Man be memory
As Plato thought: * We and pofterity

---

* It would be interefting to know where Plato has made
this fingular affertion. I fear it is more eafy to account for
Herbert's remark than to corroborate it.

34

Shall celebrate his name, and virtuous grow
Only in memory that he was fo,
And on thofe terms we may feem yet to live,
Becaufe he lived once, though we fhall ftrive
To figh away this feeming life fo faft,
As if with us 'twere not already paft.
We then are dead, for what doth now remain
To pleafe us more, or what can we call pain
Now we have loft him? And what elfe doth make
Difference in life and death, but to partake
Nor Joy nor Pain? Oh death! could'ft not fulfil
Thy rage againft us no way but to kill
This Prince in whom we liv'd? that fo we all
Might perifh by thy hand at once, and fall
Under his ruin? Thenceforth though we fhould
Do all the actions that the living would,
Yet we fhall not remember that we live,
No more than when our mother's womb did give
That life we felt not. Or fhould we proceed
To fuch a wonder, that the dead fhould breed,
It fhould be wrought to keep that memory
Which being his, can, therefore, never die.

November 9, 1612.

EPITAPH OF KING JAMES.

HERE lies King James, who did so propagate
    Unto the World that blest and quiet state
Wherein his subjects liv'd, he seemed to give
That peace which Christ did leave; and did so live,
As once that King and Shepherd of his Sheep,
That whom God saved, here he seemed to keep,
Till with that innocent and single heart
With which he first was crown'd he did depart,
To better life. Great Brittain, so lament
That Strangers more than thou may yet resent
The sad effects, and while they feel the harm
They must endure from the victorious arm
Of our King Charles, may they so long complain,
That tears in them force thee to weep again.

A VISION.

A LADY COMBING HER HAIR.

WITHIN an open curled fea of gold   **The hair.**
    A Bark of Ivory one day I faw,   **The comb.**
Which ftriking with his oars did feem to draw   The teeth **of** the comb.
Tow'rds a fair Coaft which I then did behold.   **Her fide.**

A Lady held the Stern, while her white hand,
    Whiter than either ivory or **sail**,   The cuff or fmock fleeve.
    Over the furging waves did fo prevail
That fhe had now approached near the land.   Her fhoulder.

When fuddenly, as if fhe feared fome wrack,
    And yet the Sky was fair, and Air was clear,
    And neither Rock, nor Monfter did appear   **Wart.**
Doubling the Point, **which** fpied, fhe turned **back.**

Then with **a** fecond courfe I faw her fteer,   Combing in an-other place.
    As if fhe meant to reach fome other Bay,
    Where being approached, fhe likewife turned away,
Though in the Bark fome waves now entred were.   Hairs in the comb.

37

Though varying oft her courſe at laſt I found,
　While I in queſt of the Adventure go,

She had given over combing.　The Sail took down and Oars had ceas'd to row,

And that the Bark itſelf was run aground.

Her face.　Wherewith Earth's faireſt creature I beheld,

Her hair put up and comb caſt away.　For which both Bark and Sea I gladly loſt.

　Let no Philoſopher, of Knowledge boaſt,

Unleſs that he my Viſion can unfold.

TEARS flow no more, or if you needs muſt flow,
    Fall yet more flow,
  Do not the world invade.
From ſmaller ſprings than yours rivers have grown,
    And they again a Sea have made
Brackiſh like you, and which like you hath flown.

Ebb to my heart, and on the burning fires
    Of my deſires
  Let your torrents fall.
From ſmaller Sparks than theirs ſuch ſparks ariſe
    As into flame converting all,
This world might be but my love's ſacrifice.

Yet if, the tempeſts of my ſighs, so slow
    You both muſt flow,
  And my deſires ſtill burn,
Since that in vain all help my love requires,
    Why may not yet their rages turn
To dry thoſe tears and to blow out thoſe fires ?

Italy, 1614.

DITTY

TO THE TUNE OF A CHE DEL QUANTO MIO OF PESARINO.

WHERE now fhall thefe accents go ?
　　At which creatures filent grow
While Woods and Rocks do fpeak,
　　And feem to break
Complains too long for them to hear,
Saying I call in vain : *Echo*—All in vain.
　　　: = :　　: = :　　: = :
Where there is no relief : *Ec.*—Here is no relief.

Ah why then fhould I fear
Unto her rocky heart to fpeak that grief
In whofe laments thefe bear a part ?
　　　Then, cruel heart,
　　Do but fome anfwer give.
I do but crave. = Do you forbid to live or bid to
　　live ?
　　　Echo—Live.

40

DITTY.

CAN I then live to draw that breath
 Which muſt bid farewell to thee?
Yet how ſhould death not ſeize on me?
Since abſence from the life I hold ſo dear muſt
 needs be death.

While I do feel in parting
 Such a living dying,
As in this my moſt fatal hour,
 Grief ſuch a life doth lend
As quick'ned by his power
 Even death cannot end.

I am the firſt that ever lov'd,
 He yet that for the place contends,
 Againſt true love ſo much offends
That even this way it is prov'd.

For whofe affection once is fhown,
   No longer can the World beguile;
   Who fees his penance all the while,
He holds a Torch to make her known.

You are the firft were ever lov'd,
   And who may think this not fo true,
   So little knows of love or you,
It need not otherwife be prov'd.

For though the more judicious eyes
   May know when Diamonds are right,
   There is required a greater light
Their eftimate and worth to prize.

While they who moft for beauty ftrive
   Can with no Art fo lovely grow,
   As fhe who doth but only owe
So much as true affections give.

Thus firft of Lovers I appear,
   For more appearance makes me none,
   And thus are you belov'd alone,
That are priz'd infinitely dear.

Yet, as in our Northern Clime,
  Rare fruits, though late, appear at laſt ;
  As we may ſee ſome years being paſt,
Our Orange trees grow ripe with time.

So think not ſtrange, if Love to break
  His wonted Silence now makes bold ;
  For a Love is ſeven years old,
Is it not time to learn to ſpeak ?

Then gather in that, which doth grow
  And ripen to that faireſt hand.
  'Tis not enough that trees do ſtand
If their fruit fall and periſh too.

EPITAPH OF A STINKING POET.

HERE ſtinks a Poet I confeſs,
  Yet wanting breath ſtinks ſo much leſs.

43

A DITTY TO THE TUNE OF
COSE FERITE,

MADE BY LORENZO ALLEGRE TO ONE
SLEEPING. *To be sung.*

*A*H *Wonder!*
  So fair a heaven,
  So fair, &c.

And no Star shining.
Ay me and no Star, &c.
'Tis paſt my divining.

  Yet ſtay!
May not perchance this be ſome riſing Morn
    Which in the ſcorn
Of our World's light diſcloſes
This air of violets, that ſky of roſes?

  'Tis ſo!
An oriental ſphere
Doth open and appear,
    Aſcending bright;
Then ſince thy hymen I chant
May'ſt thou new pleaſures grant,
    Admired light.

EPITAPH
ON SIR EDWARD SACKVILLE'S CHILD,
WHO DIED IN HIS BIRTH.

R EADER ! here lies a child that never cried,
    And therefore never died.
   'Twas neither old nor yong,
Born to this and the other world in one.
   Let us then ceafe to moan,
Nothing that ever died hath liv'd fo long.

KISSING.

COME hither, Womankind, and all their **worth**,
  Give me thy kiffes as I call them forth ;
Give me thy billing kifs ; that of the Dove,
   A Kifs of Love ;
The Melting Kifs, a Kifs that doth confume
   To a perfume ;
The extract Kifs, of every fweet a part ;
   A Kifs **of Art** ;
The Kifs which ever ftirs fome new delight,
   A Kifs of Might ;
The twacking fmacking Kifs, and when you ceafe,
   A Kifs of Peace ;
The Mufick Kifs, crotchet and quaver time ;
   The Kifs of Rhyme ;
The Kifs of Eloquence which doth belong
   Unto the tongue ;
The Kifs of all the Sciences in one,
   The Kifs alone.
So 'tis enough.

DITTY.

IF you refuse me once, and think again,
    I will complain.
You are deceived ; Love is no work of Art,
  It muſt be got and born,
    Not made and worn,
Or ſuch wherein you have no part.

Or do you think they more than once can die
    Whom you deny ?
Who tell you of a thouſand deaths a day,
  Like the old Poets feign,
    And tell the pain
They met but in the common way ?

Or do you think it is too ſoon to yield
    And quit the Field ?
You are deceived, they yield who firſt intreat.
  Once one may crave for love,
    But more would prove
This heart too little, that too great.

Give me then fo much love, that we may burn
  Paft all return,
Who midft your beauties, flames, and spirit live,
  So great a light muft find
   As to be blind
To all but what their fires give.

Then give me fo much love, as in one point,
  Fixed and conjoint,
May make us equal in our flames arife,
   As we fhall never ftart,
    Until we dart
Lightning upon the envious eyes.

Then give me fo much love, that we may move
  Like ftars of love,
And glad and happy times to Lovers bring,
   While glorious in one fphere
    We ftill appear
And keep an everlafting fpring.

ELEGY OVER A TOMB.

MUST I then fee, alas! eternal night
    Sitting upon thofe faireft eyes,
And clofing all thofe beams, which once did rife
    So radiant and bright,
That light and heat in them to us did prove
    Knowledge and Love?

Oh, if you did delight no more to ftay
    Upon this low and earthly ftage,
But rather chofe an endlefs heritage,
    Tell us at leaft, we pray,
Where all the beauties that thofe afhes ow'd
    Are now beftow'd?

Doth the Sun now his light with yours renew?
    Have Waves the curling of your hair?
Did you reftore unto the Sky and Air
    The red and white and blue?
Have you vouchfafed to flowers fince your death,
    That fweeteft breath?

Had not Heav'n's Lights elfe in their houfes flept,
    Or to fome private life retir'd ?
Muft not the Sky and Air have elfe confpir'd
    And in their Regions wept ?
Muft not each flower elfe the earth could breed
    Have been a weed ?

But thus enrich'd may we not yield fome caufe
    Why they themfelves lament no more,
That muft have changed courfe they held before,
    And broke their proper Laws,
Had not your Beauties giv'n their fecond birth
    To Heaven and Earth ?

Tell us, for Oracles muft ftill afcend
    For thofe that crave them at your tomb ;
Tell us, where are thofe Beauties now become
    And what they now intend ;
Tell us, alas ! that cannot tell our grief,
    Or hope relief.

1617.

EPITAPH ON SIR FRANCIS VERE.

R EADER,—
      If thou appear
   Before that tomb attention give,
      And do not fear,
      Unleſs it be to live,
   For dead is great Sir Francis Vere.

Of whom this might be ſaid, Should God ordain
   One to deſtroy all ſinners whom That One
   Redeem'd not there, that ſo **He** might atone
His choſen flock, and take from earth that ſtain
   That ſpots it ſtill, he worthy were alone
   To finiſh it, and have, when they were gone,
This world for him made Paradiſe again.

TO MRS. DIANA CECYLL.

DIANA CECYLL, that rare beauty thou doſt
       ſhow
    Is not of Milk, or Snow,
  Or ſuch as pale and whitely things do **owe**,
But an illuſtrious Oriental Bright,
 Like to the Diamond's refra<ed light,
Or early Morning breaking from the Night.

Nor are thy hair and eyes **made of** that ruddy beam
    Or golden-ſanded ſtream
  Which we find ſtill the vulgar Poet's theme,
But reverend black, and ſuch as you would ſay
 Light did but ſerve it, and **did ſhew the way**
By which at firſt night **did** precede **the day.**

Nor is that ſymmetry of parts and form divine
    Made **of one** vulgar **line,**
  Or ſuch as any know how to define,
But of proportions new, ſo well expreſt
That the perfections in **each part** confeſt
Are beauties **to themſelves** and to the reſt.

52

To Mrs. Diana Cecyll.

Wonder of all thy Sex ! let none henceforth inquire
    Why they fo much admire,
  Since they that know thee beft afcend no higher.
Only be not with common praifes wooed,
Since admiration were no longer good,
When men might hope more then they underftood.

TO HER EYES.

BLACK eyes, if you ſeem dark,
  It is becauſe your beams are deep
  And with your ſoul united keep.
  Who could diſcern
Enough into them there, might learn
  Whence they derive that mark,
    And how their power is ſuch
That all the wonders which proceed from thence,
Affecting more the mind then ſenſe,
    Are not ſo much
The works of light, as influence.

  As you then joined are
Unto the ſoul, ſo it again
By its connexion doth pertain
    To that firſt cauſe,
Who, giving all their proper **Laws,**
    By you doth beſt declare
    How he at firſt being hid

Within the veil of an eternal night,
Did frame for us a fecond light,
      And after bid
It ferve for ordinary fight.

    His image then you are ;
If there be any yet who doubt
What power it is that doth look out
    Through that your black,
He will not an example lack,
    If he fuppofe that there
    Were grey or hazel Glafs,
And that through them, though sight or soul
    might fhine,
He muft yet at the laft define
    That beams which pafs
Through black, cannot but be divine.

TO HER HAIR.

BLACK beamy hairs, which so seem to arise
    From the extraction of those eyes,
That unto you she destin-like doth spin
The beams she spares, what time her soul retires,
    And by those hallowed fires
    Keeps house all night within.

Since from within her awful front you shine,
    As threads of life which she doth twine,
And thence ascending with the fatal rays
To crown those temples, where Love's **wonders**
      wrought,
    We afterwards see brought
    To vulgar light **and praise.**

Lighten through **all** your regions, till we find
    The causes why we are grown blind,
That when we should your Glories comprehend,
Our sight recoils, and turneth back again,
    And doth, as 'twere in vain,
    Itself to you extend.

To her Hair.

Is it, becaufe paft black, there is not found
    A fix'd or horizontal bound ?
And fo as it doth terminate the white,
It may be faid all colours to infold,
    And in that kind to hold
    Somewhat of infinite ?

Or is it that the centre of our fight,
    Being veiled in its proper night,
Difcerns your blacknefs by fome other fenfe
Than that by which it doth pied colours fee,
    Which only therefore be
    Known by their difference ?

Tell us, when on her front in curls you lie,
    So diaper'd from that black eye,
That your reflected forms may make us know
That fhining light in darknefs all would find,
    Were they not upward blind
    With the Sun-beams below.

SONNET OF BLACK BEAUTY.

BLACK beauty, which above that common light,
    Whofe Power can no colors here renew
  But thofe which darknefs can again fubdue,
Doft ftill remain unvary'd to the light ?

And like an object equal to the view,
    And neither chang'd with day nor hid with night,
    When all thefe colours which the world call bright,
And which old Poetry doth fo purfue,

Are with the night fo perifhed and gone,
    That of their being there remains no mark,
Thou ftill abideft fo entirely one,
    That we may know thy blacknefs is a fpark
Of light inacceffible, and alone
    Our darknefs which can make us think it dark.

ANOTHER SONNET TO BLACK IT SELF.

THOU Black wherein all colours are compos'd,
    And unto which they all at laſt return;
Thou colour of the Sun where it both burn,
And ſhadow, where it cools; in thee is cloſ'd
Whatever nature can, or hath diſpos'd
    In any other here; from thee do riſe
Thoſe tempers and complexions which diſcloſ'd
    As parts of thee, do work as myſteries
Of that thy hidden power; when thou doſt reign
    The characters of fate ſhine in the Skies,
And tell us what the Heavens do ordain:
    But when Earth's common light ſhines to our eyes
Thou ſo retir'ſt thyſelf, that thy diſdain
    All revelation unto man denies.

THE FIRST MEETING.

A S fometimes with a Sable Cloud
    We fee the Heavns bow'd,
  And darkning all the fire,
Until the lab'ring fires they do contain
    Break forth again ;
Ev'n fo from under your black hair
  I faw fuch an unufual blaze
Lightning and fparkling from your eyes,
And with unufed prodigies
    Forcing fuch amaze,
That I did judge your empire here
Was not of love alone but fear.

But as all that is violent
Doth by degrees relent ;
So when that fweeteft face,
Growing at laft to be ferene and clear,
    Did now appear
With all its wonted heav'nly grace,

And your appeafed eyes did send
A beam from them fo foft and mild
That former terrors were exil'd,
And all that could amaze did end ;
Darknefs in me was chang'd to light,
Wonder to love, love to delight.

Nor here yet did your goodnefs ceafe
My heart and eyes to blefs,
 For, being paft all hope
That I could now enjoy a better ftate,
  An orient gate
(As if the Heav'ns themfelves did ope)
Firft found in thee, and then difclof'd
 So gracious and fweet a fmile,
That my foul ravifhed the while,
And wholly from itfelf unloof'd,
Seem'd hov'ring in your breath to rife
To feel an air of Paradife.

Nor here yet did your favours end,
For whilft I down did bend,
As one who now did mifs
A foul which grown much happier than before
 Would turn no more,
You did beftow on me a kifs,

And in that kifs a foul infufe
Which was fo fafhion'd by your mind,
And which was fo much more refin'd
   Than that I formerly did ufe,
That if one foul found joys in thee,
The other framed them new in me.

But as thofe bodies which difpenfe
Their beams, in parting hence
Thofe beams do recollect,
Until they in themfelves refumed have
    The forms they gave;
So when your gracious afpect
  From me was turned once away,
Neither could I thy foul retain
Nor you give mine leave to remain,
  To make with you a longer ftay,
Or fuffered ought elfe to appear
But your hair, night's hemifphere.

Only as we in Loadftones find
Virtue of fuch a kind,
That what they once do give,
Being neither to be chang'd by any Clime
    Or forc'd by time,
Doth ever in its fubjects live;

So though I be from you retir'd,
The power you gave yet ftill abides,
And my foul ever fo guides
By your magnetique touch infpir'd,
That all it moves, or is inclin'd,
Comes from the motions of your mind.

A MERRY RIME

MADAM, though I'm one of thofe,
    That every fpring ufe to compofe,
That is, add feet unto round profe,
Yet you a further art difclofe,
And can, as every body knows,
Add to thofe feet fine dainty toes.
Satyrs add nails, but they are fhrews.
My mufe therefore no further goes,
But for her feet craves fhooes and hofe,
Let a fair feafon add a Rofe.
While thus attir'd we'll oppofe
The tragick bufkins of our foes.
And herewith, Madam, I will clofe,
And 'tis no matter how it fhows:
All I care is, if the Child grows.

64

THE THOUGHT.

IF you do love as well as I,
   Then every minute from your heart
      A thought doth part,
And winged with defire doth fly
Till it hath met in a ftreight line
      A thought of mine,
So like to yours, we cannot know
Whether of both doth come or go,
      Till we define
Which of us two that thought did owe.

I say then that your thoughts which pafs
Are not fo much the thoughts you meant
      As thofe I fent,
For as my image in a glafs
Belongs not to the glafs you fee,
      But unto me,
So when your fancy is fo clear
That you would think you faw me there,
      It needs muft be
That it was I did firft appear.

Likewife when I fend forth a thought
My reafon tells me, 'tis the fame
    Which from you came,
And which your beauteous Image wrought.
Thus while our thoughts by turns do lead
    None can precede ;
And thus while in each other's mind
Such interchanged forms we find,
    Our loves may plead
To be of more then vulgar kind.

May you then often think on me,
And by that thinking know 'tis true
    I thought on you.
I in the fame belief will be,
While by this mutual addrefs
    We will poffefs
A love muft live, when we do die.
Which rare and fecret property
    You will confefs,
If you do love as well as I.

TO A LADY WHO DID SING EXCELLENTLY.

WHEN our rude and unfashioned words, that long
A being in their elements enjoy'd,
    Senselefs and void,
Come at last to be formed by thy tongue,
And from thy breath receive that life and place,
    And perfect grace,
That now thy power, diffus'd through all their parts,
    Are able to remove
All the obstructions of the hardest hearts,
And teach the most unwilling how to love.

When they again, exalted by thy voice,
Tun'd by thy soul, dismiss'd into the air,
    To us repair,
A living, moving, and harmonious noise,
Able to give the love they do create
    A second state,

And **charm** not only all his griefs away,
  And his defects reſtore,
But make him perfect, who, the Poets ſay,
Made all **was ever yet made** heretofore.

When again all theſe rare perfections meet,
Compoſed in the circle of thy face,
  As in their place,
So **to make up of** all **one** perfect ſweet,
Who is not then ſo raviſhed with delight,
  Ev'n of thy ſight,
That he can be aſſur'd his ſenſe is **true,**
  Or that he die, or live,
Or that he do enjoy himſelf, or you,
Or only the delights, which you did give?

MELANDER,

SUPPOS'D TO LOVE SUSAN, BUT DID LOVE ANN.

WHO doth prefume my Miftrefs's name to fcan
    Goes about more than any way he can,
Since all men **think** that **it is** *Sufan.*   *Echo*—Anne.

What fayft ?   Then tell who is as white as Swan,
While others fet by her are pale and wan ;
Then, Echo, fpeak, Is it not *Sufan?*   *Ec.*—**Anne.**

Tell, Echo, yet, who's Middle's but a fpan,
Some being grofs as bucket, round as pan ?
Say, Echo, then, Is it not *Sufan?*   *Ec.*—Anne.

Say, is fhe not foft as meal without bran ?
Though yet in great haft once from me fhe **ran,**
Muft I not however love *Sufan? Ec.*—Anne.

ECHO TO A ROCK.

THOU heaven-threatening **Rock,** gentler then
    ſhe,
       Since of my pain
    Thou ſtill more ſenſible will be,
Only when thou giv'ſt leave but to complain.
       Echo—Complain.
But thou **doſt** anſwer too, although in vain.
Thou anſwer'ſt when thou can'ſt no pity **ſhow.**
       Echo—Oh !
    What, canſt thou ſpeak and pity **too** ?
    Then yet a further favour **do,**
And tell if of my griefs **I** any **end ſhall know.**
       Echo—No.
Sure ſhe will pity **him** that loves her ſo truly.
       Echo— You lie.
Vile **Rock,** thou now grow'ſt ſo unruly,
That hadſt thou life, as thou haſt voice,
    Thou ſhouldſt die **at my** foot.
       Echo—**Die at my foot.**

Thou canſt not make me do't
Unleſs thou leave it to my choice,
Who thy hard ſentence ſhall fulfill,
When thou ſhalt ſay **I die to pleaſe her only will.**
   Echo—I will.
When ſhe comes hither, then, I pray thee, tell
Thou art my Monument, and **this my** laſt farewell.
   Echo—Well.

ECHO IN A CHURCH.

WHEN fhall my troubled foul at large
          Difcharge
The burden of her fins, oh where?
          Echo—Here.
Whence comes this voice I hear?
  Who doth this grace afford?
  If it be thou, O Lord,

Say if thou hear my prayers, when I call.
          Echo—All.
And wilt thou pity grant when I do cry?
          Echo—I.

Then though I fall,
    Thy grace will my defects fupply.
  But who will keep my foul from ill,
Quench bad defires, reform my Will?
          Echo—I will.

O may that Will and Voice be bleſt
Which yields ſuch comforts unto one diſtreſt !
More bleſſed yet, would'ſt thou thyſelf unmaſk,
Or **tell** at leaſt who undertakes this taſk.
        Echo—Aſk.

Since now with crying I am **grown** ſo weak,
I ſhall want force even to **crave thy** name.
O ſpeak before I wholly **weary** am.
        Echo—I am.

TO HIS MISTRESS FOR HER TRUE
PICTURE.

DEATH, my life's Miſtreſs, and the Sovereign Queen
    Of all that ever breath'd, though yet unſeen,
My heart doth love you beſt, yet I confeſs,
Your picture I beheld, which doth expreſs
No ſuch eye-taking beauty ; you ſeem lean,
Unleſs you're mended ſince.   Sure he did mean
No honour to you, that did draw you ſo ;
Therefore I think it falſe.   Beſides, I know
The picture Nature drew (which ſure's the beſt)
Doth figure you by ſleep and ſweeteſt reſt.
Sleep, Nurſe of our life, Care's beſt repoſer,
Nature's high'ſt rapture, and the viſion giver.
Sleep, which when it doth ſeize us, ſouls go play,
And make Man equal as he was firſt day.
Yet ſome will ſay can pictures have more life
Than the original ?   To end this ſtrife,
Sweet Miſtreſs come, and ſhew yourſelf to me
In your true form, while then I think to ſee
Some beauty Angelick, that comes to unlock
My body's priſon, and from life unfrock

My well-divorced Soul, and ſet it free
To liberty eternal : thus you ſee,
I find the Painter's error, and protect
Your abſent Beauties, ill drawn, by th'effect.
For grant it were your work and not the Grave's,
Draw Love by Madneſs then, Tyrants by Slaves,
Becauſe they make men ſuch.   Dear Miſtreſs, then,
If you would not be ſeen by owl-ey'd men,
Appear at noon i'th' Air, with ſo much light
The Sun may be a Moon, the Day a Night,
Clear to my ſoul, but dark'ning the weak ſenſe
Of thoſe, the other World's Cimmeriens,
And in your fatal robe embroidered
With Star characters, teaching me to read
The deſtiny of Mortals, while your clear brow
Preſents a Majeſty, to inſtruct me how
To love, or dread nought elſe : May your bright hair,
Which are the threads of life, fair crown'd appear,
With that your Crown of Immortality.
In your right hand, the Keys of Heaven be,
In th'other, thoſe of the Infernal Pit,
Whence none retires if once he enter it.
And here let me complain, how few are thoſe
Whoſe ſouls you ſhall from earth's vaſt dungeon looſe
To endleſs happineſs ; few that attend
You the true guide unto their journey's end.

And if old Virtue's way narrow were,
'Tis rugged now, having no passenger.
Our life is but a dark and stormy night,
To which sense yields a weak and glimmering light,
While wandering Man thinks he discerneth all
By that which makes him but mistake and fall.
He sees enough, who doth his darkness see.
These are great lights, by which less dark'ned be.
Shine then Sun-bright, or through my senses' veil,
A day star of the light doth never fail.
Shew me that goodness which compounds the strife
'Twixt a long sickness and a weary life;
Set forth that Justice which keeps all in awe
Certain and equal more than any Law;
Figure that happy and eternal Rest,
Which till man do enjoy, he is not blest;
Come and appear then, dear Soul-ravisher,
Heav'ns lightest Usher, Man's deliverer;
And do not think, when I new beauties see,
They can withdraw my settled love from thee.
Flesh-beauty strikes me not at all, I know:
When thou do'st leave them to the grave, they show
Worse than they now show thee: they shall not move
In me the least part of delight, or love,
But as they teach your power.   Be the nut brown,
The loveliest colour which the flesh doth crown,

I'll **think** it like a Nut—a fair outfide,
Within which worms and rottennefs abide;
If fair, then like the Worm itfelf to be;
If painted, like their flime and fluttery.
If any yet will think their beauties beft,
And will againft you, fpite of all, conteft,
Seize **them** with Age; fo in themfelves they'll hate
What they fcorn'd in your picture, and too late
See their fault, and the Painter's.   **Yet if this,**
Which their great'ft plague and wrinkled torture is,
Pleafe not, you may to the more wicked fort,
Or fuch as of your praifes make a fport,
Denounce an open war, fend chofen bands
Of Worms, your foldiers, to their faireft hands,
And make them leprous, fcabb'd : upon their face
Let thofe your Pioneers, Ringworms, take their place,
And fafely near with ftrong approaches got,
Intrench it round, while their teeths' rampire **rot,**
With other Worms, nay with a damp inbred,
Sink to their fenfes, which they fhall not dread.
And thus may all that ere they prided in,
Confound them now.   As for the parts within
Send great Worms, which may undermine a way
Into their vital parts, and fo difplay
That, your pale enfign on the walls; then let
Thofe worms your Veterans which never yet

Did fail, **enter** pell-mell and ransack all.
Juft **as** they fee the well-rais'd building fall.
While they do this, your Forragers command,
The Caterpillars, to devour their land,
And with them Wasps, your wing'd-worm-horsemen, bring
To charge, in troop, **those** Rebels, with their sting.
All this, unless your beauty they confess.

And now, sweet Mistress, let me awhile digress
To admire these noble Worms whom I invoke,
And not the Mufes.   You that eat through oak
And bark, **will** you spare Paper and my Verse,
Because your praises they do here rehearse?

Brave Legions then, sprung from the mighty race
Of man corrupted, and which hold the place
Of his undoubted issue: you that are
Brain-born, Minerva-like, and, like her, war,
Well arm'd, complete, mail'd-jointed soldiers,
Whose force Herculean links in pieces tears,
To you the vengeance of all Spill-bloods falls,
Beast-eating Men, Men-eating cannibals,
Death privileg'd, were you in funder smit,
You do not lose your life, but double it.
Best-framed types of the Immortal Soul,
Which in your felves, and in each part, are whole.

Last-living Creatures, heirs of all the earth,
For when all men are dead, it is your birth;
When you die, your brave self-killed General,
For nothing else can kill him, doth end all.
What vermine-breeding body then thinks scorn
His flesh should be by your brave fury torn?
Willing, to you, this carcass I submit,
A gift so free, I do not care for it,
Which yet you shall not take until I see
My Mistress first reveal herself to me.

Meanwhile, Great Mistress, whom my soul admires,
Grant me your true picture, who it desires,
That he your matchless beauty might maintain,
'Gainst all men that will quarrels entertain.
For a Flesh-Mistress, the worst I can do
Is but to keep the way that leads to you,
And howsoever the event doth prove,
To have Revenge below, Reward above.
Hear, from my body's prison, this my call,
Who from my mouth-grate and eye-window bawl.

EPITAPH ON SIR PHILIP SIDNEY,

LYING IN ST. PAUL'S WITHOUT A MONUMENT, TO BE FASTENED UPON THE CHURCH DOOR.

R EADER,—
  Within this church Sir Philip Sidney lies,
Nor is it fit that I ſhould more acquaint,
    Left Superftition rife,
    And men adore,
Soldiers, their Martyr; Lovers, their Saint.

EPITAPH FOR HIMSELF.

R EADER,—
   The Monument which thou beholdeſt here,
  Preſents Edward Lord Herbert to thy ſight,
A man, who was ſo free from either hope or fear,
   To have, or loſe this ordinary light,
That when to elements his body turned were
   He knew, that as thoſe elements would fight,
So his Immortal Soul ſhould find above
With his Creator, Peace, Joy, Faith, and Love.

SONNET.

YOU well-compacted groves, whofe light and fhade
    Mixt equally, produce nor heat nor cold,
Either to burn the young, or freeze the old,
But to one even temper being made,
Upon a Grove embroidering through each glade
An Airy Silver, and a Sunny Gold,
So clothe the pooreft that they do behold
Themfelves in riches which can never fade,
While the wind whiftles, and the birds do fing,
While your twigs clip, and while the leaves do frifs,
While the fruit ripens which thofe trunks do bring,
Senfelefs to all but love, do you not fpring
Pleafure of fuch a kind, as truly is
A felf renewing vegetable blifs ?

Made upon the Groves near Merlou Caftle.

82

TO THE C. OF D.*

SINCE in your face, as in a beauteous sphere,
    Delight and state so sweetly mix'd appear,
That Love's not light, nor Gravity severe,
All your attractive graces seem to draw,
A modest rigor keepeth so in awe,
That in their turns, each of them gives the law.

Therefore, though chaste and virtuous, desire
Through that, your native mildness, may aspire,
Until a just regard it dost acquire ;
Yet if Love thence a forward hope project
You can, by virtue of a sweet neglect,
Convert it streight to reverend respect.

Thus, as in your rare temper, we may find
An excellence so perfect in each kind,
That a fair body hath a fairer mind ;
So all the beams you diversly do dart,
As well on th'understanding as the heart,
Of love and honour equal cause impart.

---

* Possibly the Countess of Denbigh, the patroness of Carew.

DITTY.

1.

WHY doſt thou hate return inſtead of love?
And with ſuch mercileſs deſpite
My faith and hope requite?
Oh! if th'affection cannot move,
Learn innocence yet of the Dove,
And thy diſdain to juſter bounds confine.
Or if t'wards Man thou equally decline
The rules of Juſtice and of Mercy too,
Thou may'ſt thy love to ſuch a point refine
As it will kill more than thy hate can do.

2.

Love, love, Melaina, then, though death enſue,
Yet it is a greater fate
To die through love than hate.
Rather a victory purſue
To Beauty's lawful conqueſt due,

84

Than tyrant eyes envenom with difdain.
Or if thy Power thou wouldft fo maintain
As equally to be both lov'd **and** dread,
Let timely Kiffes call to life again
Him whom thine eyes have Planet-ftrucken dead.

3.

Kifs, kifs, Melaina, then, and do **not ftay**
    Until thefe fad effects appear
    Which now draw on fo near,
    That didft thou longer help delay
    My foul muft fly fo faft away
As would at once both life and love divorce ;
Or if **I** needs muft die without remorfe,
Kifs and embalm me fo with that fweet breath,
That while **thou** triumph'ft o'er Love and his force,
I may triumph yet over Fate **and Death.**

ELEGY FOR DOCTOR DUNN.*

WHAT though the vulgar **and** received praiſe
    With which each common Poet ſtrives to ɪaiſe
His worthleſs Patron, ſeem to give the height
Of **a** true excellence, yet as the weight
Forced from his centre, muſt again recoil,
So every praiſe, as if it took ſome foil
Only becauſe it was not well imploy'd,
Turns to thoſe ſenſeleſs principles and void,
Which in ſome broken ſyllables being vouched
Cannot above an Alphabet be couched,
In which diſſolved ſtate they uſed to reſt
Until ſome other in new forms inveſt
Their eaſy matter, ſtriving ſo to fix
Glory with words and make the parts to mix.

But ſince **praiſe that wants truth, like** words that want
Their proper meaning, doth it ſelf recant;
Such terms, however elevate and high,
Are but like meteors, which the pregnant Sky

---

* He will be better recogniſed as **Dr.** John Donne. He
died March 31ſt, 1631.

Varies in divers figures, till at laſt
They either be by ſome dark cloud o'recaſt,
Or wanting inward ſuſtence do devolve,
And into their firſt Elements reſolve.
Praiſes, like garments then, if looſe and wide,
Are ſubject to fall off; if gay and pied,
Make men ridiculous: The juſt and grave
Are thoſe alone which men may wear and have.

How fitting were it then each had that part
Which is their due, and that no fraudulent art
Could ſo diſguiſe the truth but they might own
Their rights, and by that property be known.
For ſince Praiſe is publick inheritance,
If any Inter-Commoner do chance
To give or take more praiſe than doth belong
Unto his part, he doth ſo great a wrong,
That all who claim an equal intereſt
May him implead until he do deveſt
His uſurpations, and again reſtore
Unto the Publick what was theirs before.

Praiſes ſhould then, like definitions, be
Round, neat, convertible, ſuch as agree
To perſons, ſo that were their names conceal'd
Muſt make them known as well as if reveal'd,

Such as contain the kind and difference
And all the properties arifing thence.
All praifes elfe, as more or lefs than due,
Will prove, or ftrangly falfe, or weakly true.

Having delivered now what praifes are,
It refts that I fhould to the world declare
Thy praifes, DUNN, whom I fo lov'd alive
That with my witty Carew I fhould ftrive
To celebrate the dead, did I not need
A language by itfelf, which fhould exceed
All thofe which are in ufe : For while I take
Thofe common words, which men may even rake
From Dunghill-wits, I find them fo defiled,
Slubber'd and falfe, as if they had exiled
Truth and propriety, fuch as do tell
So little other things, they hardly fpell
Their proper meaning, and therefore unfit
To blazon forth thy merits, or thy wit.

Nor will it ferve that thou didft fo refine
Matter with words that both did feem divine
When thy breath utter'd them, for thou being gone
They ftreight did follow thee.   Let therefore none
Hope to find out an Idiom and Senfe
Equal to thee and to thy Eminence,

Unlefs our gracious King give words their bound,
Call in falfe titles which each where are found
In Profe and Verfe, and as bad Coin and Light
Supprefs them and their values, till the right
Take place and do appear, and then in lieu
Of thofe forg'd Attributes ftamp fome anew,
Which being current and by all allow'd
In Epitaphs and Tombs might be avow'd
More then their Efcucheons.   Meanwhile, becaufe
Nor praife is yet confined to its laws,
Nor railing wants his proper dialect,
Let thy detraction thy late life detect,
And though they term all thy heat, forwardnefs,
Thy folitude, felf-pride, fafts, niggardnefs,
And on this falfe fuppofal would infer
They teach not others right, themfelves who err,
Yet as men to the adverfe part do ply
Thofe crooked things, which they would rectify,
So would perchance to loofe and wanton Man
Such vice avail more than their virtues can.

THE BROWN BEAUTY.

1.

WHILE the two contraries of Black and **White**,
  In the Brown Fay are fo well unite,
That they no longer now feem oppofite,
Who doubts **but** love hath this his colour chofe,
Since he therein doth both th'extremes compofe,
And as within their proper Centre clofe?

2.

Therefore, as it prefents not to the **view**
That whitely raw and unconcoded hue
Which, Beauty, Northern Nations think the true,
So neither hath it that aduft afpect
The Moor and Indian fo much affect,
That for it they all other do reject.

3.

Thus while the White well fhadow'd doth appear,
And black doth through his luftre grow fo clear
That each in other equal part doth bear,

All in fo rare proportion is combin'd
That the fair temper, which adorns her mind,
Is even to her outward form confin'd.

4.

Fay, **your** fexe's honour, then fo live
That when the world fhall with contention ftrive
To whom **they would** a chief perfection give,
They might the controverfy fo decide
As, quitting all extremes on either fide,
You more than any may be dignify'd.

AN ODE

UPON A QUESTION MOVED WHETHER LOVE SHOULD CONTINUE FOR EVER.

HAVING interr'd her Infant-birth,
　　The wat'ry ground, that late did mourn
Was ftrew'd with flow'rs, for the return
　　Of the wifh'd Bridegroom of the Earth.

The well-accorded Birds did fing
　　Their hymns unto the pleafant time,
　　And in a fweet conforted chime
Did welcome in the cheerful Spring.

To which, foft whiftles of the Wind,
　　And warbling murmurs of a Brook,
　　And varied notes of leaves that fhook,
An harmony of parts did bind.

While doubling joy unto each other
　　All in fo rare confent was fhown,
　　No happinefs that came alone,
Nor pleafure that was not another.

When with a love none can exprefs
  That mutually happy pair,
  Melander and Celinda fair,
The feafon with their loves did blefs.

Walking thus towards a pleafant **grove,**
  Which did, it feem'd, in new delight
  The pleafures of the time unite,
They give a triumph to their love.

They ftay'd **at** laft and on the grafs
  Repofed fo, as o're his breaft
  She bow'd her gracious head to reft,
Such a weight as no burden was.

While over either's compaff'd waift
  Their folded arms were fo compof'd
  As if in ftraiteft bonds inclof'd,
They fuffer'd for joys they did tafte.

Long their fixt eyes to Heaven bent,
  Unchanged they did never move,
  As if fo great and pure a love
No glafs but it could reprefent.

When, with a fweet though troubled look,
  She firft brake filence, faying, Dear Friend,
  O that our love might take no end,
Or never had beginning took !

I fpeak not this with a falfe heart
   (Wherewith his hand fhe gently ftrain'd),
   Or that would change a love maintain'd
With fo much faith on either part ;

Nay, I proteft ; though Death with his
   Worft Counfel fhould divide us here,
   His terrors could not make me fear
To come where your lov'd prefence is.

Only, if love's fire with the breath
   Of life be kindled, I doubt
   With our laft air 'twill be breath'd out,
And quenched with the cold of death ;

That if affection be a line
   Which is clof'd up in our laft hour,
   Oh, how 'twould grieve me, any pow'r
Could force fo dear a love as mine !

She fcarce had done, when his fhut eyes
   An inward joy did reprefent
   To hear Celinda thus intent
To a love he fo much did **prize,**

Then with a look, it feem'd deny'd
   All earthly pow'r but hers, yet fo
   As if to her breath he did owe
This borrow'd life, he thus replied :

O you, wherein, they fay, Souls reft
   Till they defcend, pure heavenly fires,
   Shall luftful and corrupt defires
With your immortal feed be bleft ?

And fhall our Love, fo far beyond
   That low and dying appetite,
   And which fo chaft defires unite,
Not hold in an eternal bond ?

It is, becaufe we fhould decline,
   And wholly from our thoughts exclude
   Objects that may the fenfe delude
And ftudy only the Divine.

No fure, for if none can afcend
   Ev'n to the vifible degree
   Of things created, how fhould we
The invifible comprehend ?

Or rather, fince that Pow'r expreft
   His greatnefs in his works alone,
   Being here beft in's Creatures known,
Why is he not lov'd in them beft ?

But is't not true, which you pretend,
   That fince our love and knowledge here,
   Only as parts of life appear,
So they with it fhould take their end ?

95

O no, Belov'd, I am moſt ſure
   Thoſe vertuous habits we acquire
   As being with the Soul entire
Muſt with it evermore endure;

For if, where ſins and vice reſide
   We find ſo foul a guilt remain,
   As never dying in his ſtain
Still puniſh'd in the Soul doth bide;

Much more that true and real joy,
   Which in a virtuous love is found
   Muſt be more ſolid in its ground
Then Fate or Death can e're deſtroy.

Elſe ſhould our Souls in vain elect,
   And vainer yet were Heaven's laws,
   When to an everlaſting Cauſe
They gave a periſhing effect.

Nor here on earth then, or above,
   Our good affection can impair,
   For where God doth admit the fair
Think you that he excludeth Love?

Theſe eyes again then eyes ſhall ſee,
   And hands again theſe hands enfold,
   And all chaſte pleaſures can be told
Shall with us everlaſting be.

For if no ufe of fenfe remain,
   When bodies once this life forfake,
   Or they **could** no delight partake,
Why fhould they ever rife again ?

And if every imperfect **mind**
   Make love the end of knowledge **here,**
   How perfect **will our love be, where**
All imperfection **is** refined !

Let then no doubt, Celinda, touch,
   Much lefs your faireft mind invade :
   Were not our fouls immortal made
Our equal loves can make them fuch.

So when one wing can make no **way**
   Two joined can themfelves dilate,
   So can **two** perfons propagate
When fingly either would decay.

So when from hence we fhall be gone,
   And be no more, nor you, nor I,
   As one another's myftery,
Each fhall be both, yet both but one.

This faid, in her uplifted face,
   Her eyes, which did that beauty **crown,**
   Were like two ftars, that having **fall'n down,**
Look up again to find their place.

While such a moveless silent peace
   Did cease on their becalmed sense,
   One would have thought some Influence
Their ravish'd spirits did possess.

THE GREEN-SICKNESS BEAUTY.

THOUGH the pale white within your cheeks
     compos'd,
And doubtful light unto your eye confin'd,
Though your short breath not from it self unloos'd,
And carelefs motions of your equal mind,
Argue your beauties are not all difclof'd,

Yet as a rifing beam, when firft 'tis fhewn,
Points fairer, than when it afcends more red,
Or as a budding rofe, when firft 'tis blown,
Smells fweeter far, than when it is more fpread,
As all things beft by principles are known,

So in your green and flourifhing eftate
A beauty is difcern'd more worthy love
Than that which further doth itfelf dilate,
And thofe degrees of variation prove,
Our vulgar wits fo much do celebrate.

99

Thus though your eyes dart not that piercing **blaze**,
Which doth in bufy Lovers' looks appear,
It is becaufe you do not need to gaze
On other objects than your proper fphere,
Nor wander further than to run that maze.

So, if you want that blood which muft **fucceed,**
And give at laft a tincture to your fkin,
It is, becaufe neither in outward deed,
Nor inward thought, you yet admit that fin,
For which your cheeks a guilty blufh fhould need.

So if your breath do not fo freely flow,
It is becaufe you love not to confume
That vital treafure, which you **do** beftow
As well to vegetate as to perfume
Your Virgin leaves, as faft as **they do grow.**

Yet ftay not here. Love for his right will call :
You were not born to ferve your **only will,**
Nor can your beauty be perpetual.
'Tis your perfection for to ripen ftill,
And to be gathered, rather than to fall.

THE GREEN-SICKNESS BEAUTY.

FROM thy pale look, while angry Love doth feem
  With more imperioufnefs to give his Law
Than when he blufhingly doth beg efteem,
  We may obferve pied beauty in fuch awe,
That the brav'ft colour under her command
  Affrighted, oft before you doth retire,
While, like a Statue of your felf, you ftand
  In fuch symmetrique form, as doth require
No luftre but his own : As then in vain
  One fhould flefh-colouring to ftatues add,
So were it to your native White a Stain,
  If it in other ornaments were clad,
Than what your rich proportions do give,
  Which in a boundlefs fair being unconfin'd,
Exalted in your foul, fo feem to live,
  That they become an emblem of your mind,
That fo, who to your Orient White fhould join
  Thofe fading qualities moft eyes adore,
Were but like one, who gilding Silver Coin,
  Gave but occafion to fufpect it more.

LA GRALLETTA GALLANTE,

OR

THE SUN-BURN'D EXOTIQUE BEAUTY.

1.

CHILD of the Sun, in whom his Rays appear
  Hatch'd to that luſtre, as doth make thee wear
Heavn's livery in thy ſkin, what need'ſt thou fear
The injury of Air, and change of Clime,
When thy exalted form is ſo ſublime
As to tranſcend all power of change or time?

2.

How proud are they that in their hair but ſhow
Some part of thee, thinking therein they owe
The greateſt beauty Nature can beſtow,
When thou art ſo much fairer to the ſight,
As beams each where diffuſed are more bright
Than their deriv'd and ſecondary light.

3.

But Thou art cordial both to fight and tafte,
While each rare fruit feems in his time to hafte
To ripen in thee, till at length they wafte
Themfelves to inward fweets, from whence again,
They, like Elixirs, paffing through each vein,
An endlefs circulation do maintain.

4.

How poor are they then, whom if we but greet,
Think that raw juice, which in their lips we meet,
Enough to make us hold their Kiffes fweet;
When that rich odour, which in thee is fmelt,
Can it felf to a balmy liquor melt,
And make it to our inward fenfes felt.

5.

Leave then thy Country, Soil, and Mother's Home,
Wander a Planet this way, till thou come
To give our Lovers here their fatal doom,
While, if our beauties fcorn to envy thine,
It will be juft they to a Jaundice pine,
And by thy Gold, fhow like fome Copper-Mine.

PLATONICK LOVE.

1.

MADAM, your beauty and your lovely parts
    Would fcarce admit poetic praife and arts,
As they are Love's moft fharp and piercing darts;
Though, as again they only wound and kill,
The more deprav'd affections of our will,
You claim a right to commendation ftill.

2.

For as you can unto that height refine
All Loves delights, as while they do incline
Unto no vice, they fo become divine,
We may as well attain your excellence,
As, without help of any outward fenfe
Would make us grow a pure Intelligence.

3.

And as a Soul, thus being quite abſtract,
Complies not properly with any act,
Which from its better Being may detract,
So, through the virtuous habits which you infuſe
It is enough that we may like and chooſe,
Without preſuming yet to take or uſe.

4.

Thus Angels in their ſtarry Orbs proceed
Unto Affection, without other need
Than that they ſtill on contemplation feed,
Though as they may unto this Orb deſcend,
You can, when you would ſo much lower bend,
Give Joys beyond what Man can comprehend.

5.

Do not refuſe, then Madam, to appear,
Since every radiant Beam comes from your Sphere,
Can ſo much more than any elſe endear,
As while through them we do diſcern each Grace
The multiplied lights from every Place,
Will turn and circle, with their rays, your face.

PLATONICK LOVE.

1.

MADAM, believe't, Love is not such a toy,
    As it is sport but for the Idle Boy,
Or wanton Youth, since it can entertain
Our serious thoughts, and make us know how vain
All time is spent we do not thus imploy.

2.

For though strong passion oft on youth doth seize
It is not yet affection, but disease ;
Caused from repletion, which their blood doth vex,
So that they love not Woman, but the Sex,
And care no more than how themselves to please.

3.

Whereas true Lovers check that appetite
Which would presume further than to invite
The Soul unto that part it ought to take,
When that from this address it would but make
Some introduction only to delight.

4.

For while they from the outward fenfe tranfplant
The love grew there in earthly mould, and fcant,
To the Soul's fpacious and immortal field,
They fpring a love eternal, which will yield
All that a pure affection can grant.

5.

Befides, what time or diftance might effect
Is thus remov'd, while they themfelves connect
So far above all change, as to exclude
Not only all which might their fenfe delude,
But mind to any object elfe effect.

6.

Nor will the proof of Conftancy be hard
When they have plac'd upon their Mind that guard
As no ignoble thought can enter there,
And Love doth fuch a Virtue perfevere,
And in it felf fo find a juft reward.

7.

And thus a love, made from a worthy choice,
Will to that union come, as but one voice,
Shall fpeak, one thought but think the other's will,
And while, but frailty, they can know no ill,
Their fouls more than their bodies muft rejoice.

8.

In which eſtate nothing can ſo fulfill
Thoſe heights of pleaſure, which their ſouls inſtill
Unto each other, but that love thence draws
New Arguments of joy, while the ſame cauſe
That makes them happy, makes them greater ſtill.

9.

So that however multiplied and vaſt
Their love increaſe, they will not think it paſt
The bounds of growth, till their exalted fire
Being equally inlarg'd with their deſire,
Transform and fix them to one Star at laſt.

10.

Or when that otherwiſe they were inclin'd
Unto thoſe publick joys, which are aſſign'd
To bleſſed Souls when they depart from hence,
They would, beſides what Heaven doth diſpenſe,
Have their contents they in each other find.

THE IDEA,

MADE OF ALNWICK IN HIS EXPEDITION TO SCOTLAND WITH THE ARMY, 1639.

ALL Beauties vulgar eyes on earth do fee,
    At beft but fome Imperfect Copies be
Of thofe the Heavens did at firft decree ;

For though th' Ideas of each fev'ral kind
Conceiv'd above by the Eternal Mind
Are fuch, as none can error in them find,

Since from his thoughts and prefence he doth bar
And fhut out all deformity fo far,
That the leaft beauty near him is a Star.

As Nature yet from far th' Ideas views,
And doth befides but vile materials choofe,
We in her works obferve no fmall abufe.

Some of her figures therefore foil'd and blurr'd,
Show as if Heaven had no way concurr'd
In fhapes fo difproportion'd and abfurd.

Which being again vex'd with fome hate and fpite
That doth in them vengeance and rage **excite,**
Seem to be tortur'd and deformed quite.

While fo being fixt, they yet in them contain
Another fort of uglinefs and ftain,
Being with old wrinkles interlin'd again.

Laftly, as if Nature ev'n did not know
What colour every fev'ral part fhould owe,
They look as if their Galls would overflow.

Fair is the Mark of Good, and Foul, of ill,
Although not fo infallibly, but ftill
The proof depends moft on the mind and will.

As Good yet rarely in the Foul is met,
So 'twould as little by its union get,
As a rich Jewel that were poorly fet.

For fince Good firft did at the Fair begin,
Foul being but a punifhment for fin,
Fair's the true outfide to the Good within.

In thefe the Supreme Pow'r then fo doth guide
Nature's weak, hand, as he doth add befide
All by which Creatures can be dignified,

While you in them fee fo exact a line,
That through each fev'ral parts a glimpfe doth fhine
Of their original and form divine.

Therefore the characters of fair and good
Are fo fet forth, and printed in their blood,
As each in other may be underftood.

That Beauty fo accompanied with Grace,
And equally confpicuous in the face,
In a fair Woman's outfide takes the place.

Thus while in her all rare perfection meets,
Each, as with Joy, its fellow beauty greets,
And varies fo into a thoufand fweets.

Or if fome tempting thought do fo affault
As doubtful fhe 'twixt two opinions halt,
A gentle blufh corrects and mends the fault.

That fo fhe ftill fairer, and better grows,
Without that thus fhe more to paffion owes
Than what frefh colour on her cheeks beftows.

To which again her lips fuch helps can add
As both will chafe all grievous thoughts and fad,
And give what elfe can make her good or glad.

111

As Statuaries, yet having fram'd in Clay
An hollow image, afterwards convey
The molten metal through each feveral way,

But when it once unto its place hath paft,
And th'inward Statua perfectly is caft,
Do throw away the outward Clay at laft.

So when that form the Heavns at firft decreed
Is finifhed within, Souls do not need
Their Bodies more, but would from them be freed.

For who ftill cover'd with their earth would lie?
Who would not fhake their fetters off and fly,
And be at leaft, next to a Deity?

However then you be moft lovely here,
Yet, when you from all Elements are clear,
You far more pure and glorious fhall appear.

Thus from above I doubt not to behold
Your fecond felf renew'd in your own mold,
And rifing thence fairer then can be told.

From whence afcending to the Elect and Bleft
In your true Joys you will not find it leaft
That I in Heav'n fhall know, and love you beft.

For while **I** do your coming there attend,
I ſhall much **time on** your Idea ſpend,
And note how far you all others tranſcend.

And thus, though you more than an angel be,
Since being here to Sin and Miſchief free,
You will have raiſ'd your ſelf to their degree,

That ſo, victorious over Death and Fate,
And happy in your everlaſting ſtate,
You ſhall triumphant enter Heaven gate.

Haſten not thither yet, for as you are
A Beauty upon Earth without compare,
You will ſhew beſt ſtill where you are moſt rare.

Live all our lives then ; If the picture can
Here entertain a loving abſent Man,
Much more the Idea whence you firſt began.

PLATONICK LOVE.

DISCONSOLATE and fad,
 So little hope of remedy I find
That when my matchlefs Miftrefs were inclin'd
To pity me, 'twould fcarcely make me glad,
The difcompofing of fo fair a mind
Being that which would to my Afflictions add.

  For when fhe fhould repent,
This Act of Charity had made her part
With fuch a precious Jewel as her Heart,
Might fhe not grieve that e'er fhe did relent?
And then were it fit I felt the fmart
Until I grew the greateft penitent.

  Nor were't a good excufe,
When fhe pleaf'd to call for her Heart again,
To tell her of my fuffering and pain,
Since that I fhould her Clemency abufe,
While fhe did fee what wrong fhe did fuftain,
In giving what fhe juftly might refufe.

Vex'd thus with me at laſt,
When from her kind reſtraint ſhe now were gone,
And I left to the Manacles alone,
Should I not on another Rock be caſt?
Since they who have not yet content, do moan
Far leſs than they whoſe hope thereof is paſt?

Beſides I would deſerve,
And not live poorly on the alms of **Love**,
Or claim a favour did not ſingly move
From my regard : if ſhe her joys reſerve
Unto ſome other, ſhe at length ſhould prove,
Rather than beg her pity I would ſtarve.

Let her then be ſerene,
Alike exempt from pity and from hate,
Let her ſtill keep her dignity and ſtate,
Yet from her glories ſomething I ſhall glean,
For when ſhe doth them everywhere dilate
A beam or two to me muſt intervene.

And this ſhall me ſuſtain,
For though due merit I cannot expreſs,
Yet ſhe ſhall know none ever lov'd for leſs
Or eaſier reward. **Let** her remain
Still great and good, and from her Happineſs
My chief contentment I will entertain.

Reſtrained hopes, though you dare not aſpire
To fly an even pitch with my deſire,
Yet fall no lower, and at leaſt take heed
That you no way **unto** deſpair proceed,
Since in what form ſo'er you keep **entire**
I ſhall the leſs all other comforts need.

I know **how** much preſumption did tranſcend,
When that affection could at moſt pretend
To be believ'd, would needs yet higher ſoar
And love a Beauty which I ſhould adore,
Though **yet therein I had** no other end,
But to aſſure that none could love her more.

Only may ſhe not think her beauty leſs
That on low **objects it doth** ſtill expreſs
An equal force, **while it doth** rule all hearts
Alike in the remot'ſt as neareſt parts,
Since if it did at any diſtance **ceaſe**
It wanted of that pow'r it ſhould impart.

Small earthly lights but to ſome ſpace **extend,**
And then unto the dim and dark do tend,
And common heat doth at ſome length ſo ſtop
That it cannot ſo much as warm one drop,
While light and heat that doth from Heav'n deſcend
Warms the low Valley more than the Mountain top.

Nor do they always beſt of the Heav'ns deſerve,
Who gaze on't moſt, but they who do reſerve
Themſelves to know it, ſince not all that will
Climb up into a Steeple or a Hill
So well its pow'r and influence obſerve,
As they who ſtudy and remark it ſtill.

Would ſhe then in full glory on me ſhine,
An Image of that Light which is divine,
I then ſhould ſee more clear, while ſhe did draw
Me upwards, and the vapors twixt us awe.
To open her eyes, were to open mine,
And teach her wonders which I never ſaw.

Nor would there thus be any cauſe to fear,
That while her pow'r attractive drew me near,
The odds betwixt us would the leſſer ſhow,
Since the moſt common Underſtandings know
That inequalities ſtill moſt appear,
When brought together and compoſed ſo.

As there is nothing yet doth ſo excell,
But there is found, if not its parallel,
Yet ſomething ſo conform, as though far leaſt
May yet obtain therein an Intereſt,
Why may not faith and truth then join ſo well
As they may ſuit her rare perfections beſt ?

Then, hope, fuſtain **thy** ſelf; though thou art hid
Thou liveſt ſtill, **and** muſt till ſhe forbid ;
For when ſhe would my vows and love rejeƈt,
They would **a Being in** themſelves projeƈt,
Since infinites **as** they, yet never did,
Nor could conclude without ſome good effeƈt.

A MEDITATION

UPON HIS WAX-CANDLE BURNING OUT.

WHILE thy ambitious flame doth ſtrive for height,
    Yet burneth down as clogged with the weight
Of earthly parts, to which thou art combin'd,
Thou ſtill doſt grow more ſhort of thy deſire,
And doſt in vain unto that place aſpire
    To which thy native powers ſeem inclin'd.

Yet when at laſt thou com'ſt to be diſſolv'd,
And to thy proper principles rèſolv'd,
    And all that made thee now is diſcompoſ'd,
Though all thy terreſtrial part in aſhes lies,
Thy more ſublime to higher Regions flies,
    The reſt being to the middle ways expoſ'd.

And while thou doeſt thy ſelf each where diſperſe
Some parts of thee make up this Univerſe,
    Others a kind of dignity obtain,
Since thy pure Wax, in its own flame conſum'd,
Volumes of incenſe sends, in which perfum'd
    Thy ſmoak mounts where thy fire could not attain.

More more our Souls then, when they go from hence,
And back unto the Elements difpenfe,
   All that built up our frail and earthly frame
Shall through each pore and paffage make their breach,
Till they with all their faculties do reach
   Unto that place from whence at firft they came.

Nor need they fear thus to be thought unkind
To thofe poor Carcafes they leave behind,
   Since being in unequal parts commix'd
Each in his Element their place will get;
And who thought Elements unhappy yet
   As long as they were in their ftations fix'd?

Or if they fally forth, is there not light
And heat in fome, and fpirit prone to fight?
   Keep they not in Earth and Air the field?
Befides, have they not pow'r to generate
When more than Meteors they Stars* create,
   Which while they laft, fcarce to the brighteft yield?

That fo in them we more than once may live,
While thefe materials which here did give
   Our bodies effence, and are moft of ufe,
Quick'ned again by the world's common foul,
Which in it felf and in each part is whole,
   Can various forms in divers kinds produce.

---

* In the Conftellation of Caffiopeia, 1572.

If, then, at worſt, this our condition be
When to themſelves the Elements are free,
 And each doth to its proper place revert,
What may we not hope from our part divine
Which can this droſs of Elements refine
 And them unto a better ſtate aſſert?

Or if as clods upon this earthly ſtage,
Which repreſents nothing but change or age,
 Our ſouls would all their burdens here diveſt,
They ſingly may that glorious ſtate acquire,
Which fills alone their infinite deſire
 To be of perfect happineſs poſſeſt.

And therefore I who do not live and move
By outward ſenſe ſo much as faith and love,
 Which is not in inferior Creatures found,
May unto ſome immortal ſtate pretend,
Since by theſe wings I thither may aſcend
 Where faithful loving Souls with joys are crown'd.

OCTOBER 14, 1664.

ENRAGING Griefs, though you moſt divers be,
    In your firſt cauſes you may yet agree
To take an equal ſhare within my heart,
Since, if each grief ſtrive for the greateſt part,
You needs muſt vex yourſelves as well as me.

For your own ſakes and mine then make an end.
In vain you do about a Heart contend,
Which, though it ſeem in greatneſs to dilate,
Is but a tumor, which in this its ſtate
The choiceſt remedies would but offend.

Then ſtorm't at once.   I neither feel conſtraint,
Scorning your worſt, nor ſuffer any taint,
Dying by multitudes, though if you ſtrive,
I fear my heart may thus be kept alive,
Until it under its own burden faint.

What is't not done ?   Why then my God, I find,
Would have me ufe you to reform my mind,
Since through his help I may from you extract
An effence pure, fo fpriteful and compact
As it will be from groffer parts refin'd.

Which being again converted by his grace
To godly forrow, I may both efface
Thofe fins firft cauf'd you, and together have
Your pow'r to kill turn'd to a pow'r to fave,
And bring my Soul to its defired place.

IN STATUAM LIGNEAM OVERBURII.

CERNIS Overburi, non ære aut marmore, vultum
  Sed Ligno Hiberno dic, age, nonne placet ?

DE C. DE S.

HÆC anima, ut fuerit terrenâ libera mole,
  Venerit et fummo confpicienda Deo,
Talibus et tantis vitiis fpurcata, trahetur,
  Haud dubium, ad pœnam fuppliciumque grave.
Viderit : at pulchrum dabitur cum fumere corpus,
  Eximium, credo, perdere nollet opus.

EPITAPHIUM *IN ANAGRAMMA NOMINIS* SUI,
REDDOR UT HERBÆ.

QUAS turgens flos mane decet, quas aruit omnes
    Una dies, quas **morte** cita, nova **vita** fequetur,
Non unquam moritura **tamen,** fic *Reddor* **ut** *Herbæ.*

EPITAPH.
IN SE ROMÆ FACTUM 1615.

VEROS ceu **varios** populi ridere timores
    Expertus, vitæ melioris confcius, intus
Plaudebam, expe&tans **faceret dum fabula finem.**

IN TUMULUM DOMINI FRANCISCI VERE.

ANGUSTUS nimis eft lapis pufillus,
    Vel, totum, foret ipfa terra, marmor ;
Angufta et fpolia et Trophæa ficta,
Hæc Belgæ tulerant, vel illa Iberi.
Cuncta angufta nimis videntur illi,
Qui victor toties mori volebat,
In fe poft alios, agens triumphum,
Ut dignum tumulum, Trophæa digna
Uni nil poterit referre vero.
Ni forte, ut maneat perenne nomen
Cui mundus fpolia, et caro triumphus,
Cælum fit Tumulus, Trophœa ftellæ.

IN DIEM NATALITIUM,

VIZ. 3 MAR.

VERE novo lux uſque redit quâ naſcor, at una
    Dum tempus redit, et fit numeroſa dies,
Ver olim vires renovans, roburque recondens
    Ætas fit tandem, triſtis hyemſque mihi.

FOR A DIAL.

DISCURRENS dubiæ, placidus compendia vitæ,
    Excipiens tacito gaudia tuta ſinu,
Præteritis lætare bonis, nec ſæva futuri
    Exagitet miſeros cura premave dies.

Omnis in adverſum ruit hora, volatque retrorſum
    Et velut exhorrens jam peritura fugit.
Dum numerans delet, dumque addens ſubtrahit, illa,
    Quæ vitæ ratio, calculus atque tuæ.

IN ANSWER TO THE VERSES OF GUIET
FOR THE PUCELLE D'ORLEANS, QUASI
EXTEMPORE.

QUOD nequiere viri, potuit fi fœmina, quid ni
    Galle, fores tandem tu muliere minor?
Define, Galle, tuam tandem jactare Bubulcam,
    Seu Medæa fuit, five Medufa fuit.
Si canit ad Bellum, tamen eft Medæa vocanda,
    Carmina dum rauco concinit illa fono.
Hoftes fi cæfi, tamen eft dicenda Medufa,
    Dum nimis ad diræ virginis ora rigent.
Virgo fit tandem fed qualem nollet adulter,
    Seu Medæa fuit, five Medufa fuit.
Definat ergo fuam Gallus jactare *Johannam,*
    Saltem plena fuo non erit illa Deo.
Plena fuo vel nulla datur, vel Papa *Johanna,*
    Numine ; fit virgo quam licet illa minus.

IN ANSWER TO TILENUS
WHEN I HAD THAT FATAL DEFLUXION IN MY HAND.

QUÎ poffim Phœbum fuccenfum credere?
    Laudes
Quum facit ut fcribas, Docte Tilene, meas.
Providus atque manum confulto furripit iftam
    Ut melius poffem nunc fupereffe tuâ.

DE HUGONE GROTIO,
ARCÂ INCLUSO ET A CARCERE LIBERATO.

CARCERE dum Carcer victus, Tenebrifque Tenebræ
    Vinclis cum demum vincla foluta tibi
Profiliens mediâ tandem de mole, videris
    Quidquid mortale eft, depofuiffe fimul.

PRO LAUREATO POETA.

AT quorfum Juvenis, fi nullo limine claufus,
Immiftus canibus, faltuque vagatus in **omni**
Præcipites crebris damas latratibus urgens
Excurrit, fecumque nihil non perdere tentat?
An mage grata viri tandem maturior ætas?
Qui **furiis** agitatus, atrox, atque omine trifti
Horrida funeftis meditatur prælia campis? ﬡ
In propriam fpeciemque ruens ita fanguine gaudet
Confeffus fatis, ut nullus fibi concidat hoftis.
Is potiorne domi qui futilis ambit honorem,
Inque leves populi gyros proclivis et auram,
Mercatur voces, falfàque cupidine tractus,
Incertam dubii fectatur nominis umbram?
Heu fugias qui te fugiunt, et ferre recufant
Imperium fafcefque tuos, quibus undique fauftis
Candida fupremos defignant colla triumphos.
Sed ne **nulla** tibi demum victoria conftet,
En prædam, formofa, tuam, quam porrigit herba,
Et genua amplectens, fefe ultro dedere victam
Teftatur, lauroque fuâ tua tempora **cingit.**

Nec canos caufere meos (qui fymbola certa
Sunt fidei), tantâ folitum flammâve tremorem,
Immo nec errones tanquam, fed lumina fixa
Contemplare oculos tandem, neque bafia fpernas
Floridus ut defit color ori, fervat odorem,
Æmula paftillis fpirabunt labra rofatis
Bafia, mellito et fe lingua madore refolvet.
Denique feu noftro latitet nova pruna colore,
Nictet et implexus torvo fub lumine cautus
Arcitenens, mortis tandem feu fcena futuræ
Prodierim, vitam nobis dum dura negaris;
Ah! reddas faltem, nondum fatis arfit Amorem,
Cui fenium tempusve fidem cui præripit ullum.

AD SERENISS. REGEM GUSTAVUM,

A.D. 1631.

PER varios terræ tractus & diffita Regna,
    Inclyte Suedorum princeps, dum caftra movere
Conftituis, pacemque pio decernere bello,
Quæ te fecurum probitas, prudentia fortem,
Felicem virtus præftat, non omine vano
Fecit, ut antiquum Germania libera nomen
Accipiens rurfus **fe jufto vindice tandem**
Gaudeat, inque tuos fuccedat fponte triumphos.
Scilicet hoc potuit tua dextera fortis & ultrix,
Igneus atque vigor bello famiatus, & enfis
Quo ftricto late rutilanteque, fulgidus hoftes
Irruis in medios, denfam paffimque caternam
Difcutis, & longe percellis quæque timore,
Ut tibi nec fumi nubes glomerata, nec imo
Excuffus **pulvis**, pila nec confertior inftans
Obfcurare tuos validos, vel flectere, greffus
Poffint, è multo quin numine flamma corufcans
Perftringenfque oculos, infultus reddat inanes

Militis, innocuofque i&tus, ac irrita tela,
Dum tibi luftratæ cæcæ patuere tenebræ,
Inque tuam lucem caligo cedere vifa eft.
Inde citata tuum fequitur vi&toria curfum,
Inque gradus hæret certos figitque trophæa,
Aufpiciifque tuis illuftrior explicat alas ;
Queîs furfum ve&to, fuperas invifere fedes,
Inque novum tandem liceat tibi fidus abire
Clarius Ar&turi, et fufcæ jubar addere luci.

EURYALE MŒRENS.

DEPRESSÆ valles piceis irriguæ fontibus,
    Herbæ marcidæ, cæca prætexentes Barathra,
Maligni colles hirfutis vepribus obfiti,
Afpera montium juga, exefis hiulca fpecubus,
Defrugatarum fegetum **late** patentia æquora,
Invifa Soli antra, confragofa præcipitia,
Abruptarum cautium nutantia undique cacumina,
Pendulæ taxi, cupreffis fuccrefcentes feralibus,
  Spelæorum inferna ducentium horrores facri,
  Infauftæ ftryges, bubulantia ftygiæ avis omina,
  Rauci ftridores, torvorum colla anguium fibila,
  Prodigialium monftrorum exerta paffim capita,
  Afpectus truces fiderum, diri portenta ætheris,
  Vofque gementes umbræ, hic teftari liceat,
  Nihil ufpiam fuiffe Euryale triftius.

1632

MENSA LUSORIA;
OR, A SHOVEL-BOARD-TABLE TO MR. MASTER.*

ROBORIS excelfi tabulatum fternitur ingens,
    Æquore productum levi, quod tramite recto
Procurrens, tandem quâ fe fubducit in imum
Diffecat exilis tranfverfim linea, fcena
Unde patet ludi, commiffo margine claufa,
Qui bini ternive notam certantibus aptat
Figitur extremo, feu preffus limite jactus,
Seu tremulus nutat, fibi nec conftare videtur.
Hic ubi conveniunt lufores, quifque monetam
Argento cufam, difci formâque nitentem
Librat in adverfam, quâ ducitur orbita, partem
Perpetuo jactu, fed quæ, fi forte feratur
Plus jufto, cadit in foveam, quæ limine fummo
Cernitur, at citra feptum fi tarda fatifcit,
Rejicitur jactus, totus fit & irritus inde.
Aft intra juftam datur ut confiftere metam
Promovet hic jactum, promotum dimovet ille.
Adjicit hic alium, fed quem depellere tentat
Nonnullus ; Nummos hic obfidet, impetit ille,
Obliquo Curfu : Multâ cadit ifte ruinâ,
Dum complexa fuo funduntur fingula nexu,
Et variata vices rerum fors undique verfat.
Ludere fic liceat manibus, fic ludere mufâ,
A ftudiis feffi quum jam deceffimus ambo.

---

* Thomas Mafter, "efteemed," fays Anthony Wood, "as a vast scholar, a general artift and linguift, a noted poet, and a moft florid preacher," was a fenior ftudent of Chrift Church. He affifted Herbert in collecting materials for the *Hiftory of Henry VIII.* He died in 1643.

CHARISSIMO, DOCTISSIMO,
JUCUNDISSIMOQUE JUXTIM AMICO
THOMÆ MASTER.

Hoc Epitaph. mærens P. C. E. B. Herbert de Cherbury, 1643.

QUI fis vel fueras, Amate Mafter,
　　Lectorem fatis hæc docere poffunt ;—
Quod terris fuit ut molefta vita,
Te dempto, mage fit molefta longe,
Quod Cœlum fuit ut beata fedes,
Auctum te, mage fit beata fedes.
In terris quid agis fide vacillans ?
Si vita probus es, fruere, Lector,
Cœlo jam folito beatiore,
Mafter jam reliquis alacriore.
　Vivat in æternum virtus ac diffita terræ
　Luftret, ubique gravi fub Religione refurgens.